Jess Mowry

Simon & Schuster Books for Young Readers

ALSO BY JESS MOWRY

Rats in the Trees
Children of the Night
Way Past Cool
Six Out Seven
Ghost Train

SIMON & SCHUSTER BOOKS FOR YOUNG READERS
An imprint of Simon & Schuster Children's Publishing Division
1230 Avenue of the Americas, New York, New York 10020
Copyright © 1997 by Jess Mowry
SIMON & SCHUSTER BOOKS FOR YOUNG READERS
is a trademark of Simon & Schuster.
Book design by Symon Chow
The text for this book is set in Cochin
Printed and bound in the United States of America
First Edition
10 9 8 7 6 5 4 3 2 1
Library of Congress Cataloging-in-Publication Data
Mowry, Jess, 1960–
    Babylon boyz / by Jess Mowry. — 1st ed.
        p.   cm.
    Summary: Inner-city teenagers find a suitcase full of cocaine and must decide whether
to sell it and take the opportunities the money would provide or to destroy it to keep the
drug from poisoning their community.
    ISBN 0-689-80839-9
    [1. Inner cities—Fiction. 2. Cocaine—Fiction. 3. Drug abuse—Fiction.
4. City and town life—Fiction. 5. Afro-Americans—Fiction.] I. Title.
PZ7.M86655Bab 1997
[Fic]—dc20 96-15645

To Apollo,
for carrying on the fight

1

"Hey, homo!"

The boy tensed like a drive-by target. He scoped the scene in a glance, then spun like a dancer and leaped with an arm reaching skyward. The ball came out of the sun; a wild overshoot past the backboard. The boy's strong fingers made a casual capture and he landed lightly in big battered Cons on dry yellow grass. His grin was a secret sign flashed to his friends as he turned from the taunts being howled at him from the court. Then he tossed the ball over his shoulder like trash. It arced easily over the backboard and dropped without skin through the hoop. The curses cut off like an A.K. cleaning its clip, replaced by mutters of reluctant respect. But the boy didn't look back, just grinned again at his homeys. The other two boys only smiled as if at some dirty old joke, then all faced the school yard fence and went on with their slow walk to nowhere.

"Pook!"

The trio paused as Coach came puffing across the dead weeds and dust that passed for a playing field. Again the boys exchanged secret smiles, which probably looked more like smirks to the man. Coach was big, brown, and beer-bellied, stuffed in a rat-colored tracksuit streaked with heavy sweat stains.

The boys waited chill. All wore just faded green gym shorts, and their black and brown bodies glowed warm in the sun. But their faces went cold, showing nothing, and there was no nervous shuffle of Nikes and Cons that might have betrayed an emotion.

"Carefully, Coach, y'all have you a coronary."

It was the boy who had jumped, now standing between his two friends. Newly fourteen, he was tallest, and his hard-muscled body could have been sculpted from coffee-brown bronze. His shoulders were wide, his biceps big, and his pecs high and jutting like a pair of small bricks. His torso tapered to a slender waist below an arch of rib cage and a washboard stomach. His hands were strong and sinewed. He held them half-curled to make instant fists. His face had fierce cheekbones, a sharp jawline, a small pug nose, and above a high forehead his hair was a natural Afroish bush. His amber eyes were deep-set beneath sooty brows. His mouth was proportioned to the leanness of his jaw, but full lips sometimes made him look sulky. If his face had a flaw, it was somehow because of the teeth . . . too white, too big, and too often showing, as if his lips could cover them only with conscious effort. He showed them now: the smile of a panther, which is not a smile but a warning.

Maybe Coach caught the clue, because he stopped a few paces away from the boys and seemed to avoid the muscled one's eyes.

"Look, I'm sorry for what the guys said, Pook. It's hot, it's June, and they're . . . just being boys."

Pook stretched casually, his muscles rippling with a natural grace that no bench-built body could match. The small sapphire stud in his left earlobe winked in the sun like a tiny blue spark. The boy was too beautiful, and the man couldn't watch him without somehow being afraid.

"Look. That was a fantastic shot, Pook. Why don't you come over and get in the game? There's no reason you always got to be out here walkin' laps."

With THEM!

The last two words didn't need to be spoken. They hung in the air like stink from a Dumpster. The boys traded smirks of contempt. Coach's eyes went to the one on the right and he let his disgust drop its mask.

Wyatt might have been the fattest fourteen-year-old in all of Oaktown. He was about three hundred pounds of chocolate-brown blubber that bulged in loose rolls at his waist and hung down in front halfway to his knees. Above his huge middle were more floppy rolls and a chest like a big bobbing pair of water balloons. His face was round and chubby, wide-lipped and -nosed, and his eyes were a deep coffee color and usually friendly. His hair was woven in braids that just brushed his shoulders. A slim silver chain encircled his neck, and a tiny replica of a Krylon can dangled between the soft masses that passed for his pecs.

Coach often dissed Wyatt because the only thing wrong with fat kids was that they chose to be non-physically-motivated. He jerked a thumb toward the fence. "Keep walkin', blubber-butt!"

Wyatt didn't move; just grinned and slapped his stomach, which rippled and jiggled like Jell-O. "Free Willy!"

Coach's scowl deepened, but he forced his eyes back to Pook. "I've seen you play, son. You're *good!* That's all that matters in the game. And . . . there's really nothing wrong with you."

Pook's grin widened to show even more teeth. "Suuuure there is, Coach. I can't even *think* straight!"

Coach winced, and the boy on Pook's left started to snicker. Pook's big chest heaved in a movie-set sigh. "Oh, pleeeze, Coach! I wanna get all hot an' sweaty chasin' air-filled objects around! That make me a *real* boy!"

Coach's mud-colored cheeks took on a pink tone. "Just what in hell *do* you want to be?"

Pook's grin faded, though his lips wouldn't close all the way. "A *doctor,* you wack-ass ole fool!"

Coach's eyes narrowed, but he fought back his anger. "Uh-huh! And just where *you* gonna get the money for medical school, cupcake? You figure all them *A*'s and *B*'s in *this* suckhole gonna score you points in the real game? Hell, you can slide through here with a *B* average by just not pullin' a gun on your teacher! An', *you're* a fool if you think them college admissions people don't know that! You'd be a natural for a basketball scholarship if you'd make the right choice!"

Pook only smiled his smile that wasn't and stepped forward a pace. He held out his hand and made a casual fist, showing scarred knuckles. "This show you what choices I got?"

Coach was easily twice Pook's size, but he took a step back. These boys bothered him because they couldn't be bullied or brainwashed into being team players: Wyatt wasn't ashamed of his weight, and Pook defied every traditional rule in the book. In a last-ditch effort to save at least one, Coach turned to the boy on Pook's left. "Dante? Why don't *you* come over and get in the game? You don't belong with these losers."

Thirteen, Dante's body was wiry and lean with every small muscle tightly defined under smooth skin the shade of a moonless midnight. His torso was long, so that old T-shirts never quite covered his middle and jeans clung low on his small hips and bottom. His hands were slim, with delicate fingers that might have been able to spin silken webs. His soot-colored hair was a jungle of dredlocks that trailed down his back and over the gently squared plates of his chest. A necklace was also displayed there: bright beads of red, yellow, and green. The dreds framed an angular, finely-jawed face and shadowed large eyes the blackest of blacks, which seemed almost half-hidden by long silky lashes. His nose was a small-bridged snub above pouty lips that could easily smile, and his feet looked lion-cub large in big battered Nikes. Except for his wild Rasta mane, he seemed all Afro-American male and fit to be cast in most of the roles that young black men were expected to play. Maybe it took the wiser eyes of his homeys to see what Coach couldn't? Even then it was hard to describe, but

Pook had once said it best . . . Dante looked sort of *scuffed;* worn down from too many games like a favorite old B-ball.

Pook draped a hard-muscled arm over Dante's shoulders and aimed eyes like amber lasers at Coach. "What you all about, fool? He don't got no choice at all!"

Ignoring Pook, Coach studied the wiry midnight-black boy as if judging a pork chop. "I know what your record says, son. But, maybe you just need to exercise more? Your heart's just a muscle, and muscles get stronger with exercise."

Wyatt waddled over to stand next to Dante. "Yo, beef-brain! Your *mind's* just a muscle, an' it prob'ly ain't never been exercised since you was housebroke!"

Pook touched Dante's chest, spreading strong fingers as if to protect what beat underneath. "Hearts like his don't get no better! He need a operation, not a bunch of bullshit from some Buster Brown blowhole like you!"

Coach clenched his big fists. "Shut up, you . . . !" He took a deep breath then turned back to Dante, who looked like a pouty little black lion with an oversized mane. "So, why don't you have that operation, son? You can't improve your self-esteem without life-quality enhancement."

Dante frowned. "'Cause operations cost money! Just like everythin' else entrance you in Babylon!"

Coach snorted. "Aw, don't try pullin' that phony, Rastafarian, 'Babylon-stands-for-the-root-of-all-evil' bull crap on me! An' don't try to justify yourself as 'culturally victimized,' either. There's help you can get if you'd explore your social-assistance choices."

Dante spit on the ground. "'Choices,' hell! My dad *work* for a livin'! He choose bein' a black man, an' black men don't beg!"

Coach glanced down at his shoe: Dante had missed, but not by much. "What about Children's Hospital?"

Dante made a face. "I been on the waitin' list all my life."

Pook nodded. "They don't call what he got 'life-threatenin'.'"

"Yeah," Dante added. "You been snoopin' my records, you oughta know that. They told me if I take real good care of myself, I might even live to be thirty!" Then he smiled and touched Pook's shoulder. "Pook gonna do my operation. When he a doctor."

Shouts and curses carried from the court, where a fight had started. Coach spun around. "Damn!" Then he glanced back at Dante. "You best take *real* good care of yourself, then, boy . . . if you gonna wait for *him* to help you!" His eyes shifted to Pook and he let out a snort of disgust. "An' I sure don't know what God was thinkin' when he gave someone like *you* a body like that!" He broke into a clumsy run for the court.

"Ole wack sufferin' from rectal-cranial inversion," muttered Pook.

"Huh?" said Wyatt.

"Got his head up his ass."

"Oh." Wyatt grinned. "Gots hydrophobia too."

"*Homo*phobia."

"Naw, hydrophobia. Sucka still wet."

"Mmm." Pook looked down at himself, then turned to Dante. "Um . . . what he say, 'bout God . . . ?"

Dante smiled. "Jah don't make mistakes, homey."

"Naw," added Wyatt. "But He like a good joke once in a while."

"Oh, shut up," said Pook. Then he faced Dante again. "You okay, man? Ole fool didn't jack up your blood pressure or nuthin'?"

Dante shrugged. "Take a lot more'n his dissin' to drop me." He shook back his dreds, and a glitter of gold caught the sun from the ring in his ear. "C'mon, crew. Coach gonna be spendin' the rest of this period dealin' with that fight. We can go chill behind the backstop till the bell."

The boys continued their walk to the fence. Their pace seemed set to the slow steps of Wyatt, but it was Dante who wiped sweat from his face and sucked breath through his teeth as they crossed the dusty baseball diamond and slipped into the slim strip of shade behind the backstop. He sank down against the rotten old boards. Pook knelt quickly beside him.

"Put your head between your knees, man. It help."

Dante lowered his head, the long dreds hiding his face. "Yeah. Thanks."

Again, Pook put his palm to Dante's chest. "You gonna get a 'tack?"

"I don't think so. Just need to chill a minute, is all."

Wyatt stood, looking through the backstop's rusty mesh toward the court, where fists were still flying despite frantic blasts of Coach's whistle. "Dante right. Ole blowhole ain't gonna get them player-boys peaced 'fore the bell." He plopped down in a roly-poly heap beside Dante and blew out a satisfied sigh.

Dante's breath was coming a little easier now. "Wonder what they fightin' over today?"

Wyatt shrugged. "What boys *always* fightin' over . . . nuthin'!"

Pook rose to a crouch to scope the court, then made a disgusted sound and sat down again. Wyatt kick-backed with his arms behind his head and his stomach like a blubbery pillow filling his lap. Pook glanced around, then his bright amber eyes went to the street beyond the barbwire and chain-link school fence.

"Look like our little homeless brutha back again."

Dante raised his head and brushed back his locks. It was about fifty feet from the backstop to the fence, where a small figure stood on the sidewalk outside, fingers clutching the mesh, gazing in at the boys. "Poor little B," Dante murmured.

Wyatt shrugged. "Just another little black ant waitin' to get stepped on."

"Oh, shut up," muttered Pook. "Nobody his age choose bein' homeless."

Dante was still studying the kid. "Ever check how he look sorta . . . different? Like he be from somewheres else?"

"Bet he *wish* he somewheres else," said Wyatt. He gave the

kid a glance. "He do look kinda strange. 'Course, *you* prob'ly look a little strange too if your address be the Dumpster Hotel." Wyatt gave the kid a more critical scoping. "Axe me, he been eatin' regular. Swear he get fatter every day."

"So do you," grinned Pook.

"Oh, shut up."

Pook gazed at the kid for a moment. "Funny, I think I seen him before. Someplace else."

Dante crossed his arms on his knees and rested his chin on top, studying the kid outside the fence. "Don't think I forget seein' a brutha like that." He glanced at Wyatt. "Check out his clothes, all dirty an' old. Maybe he eatin' at one of them new malnutrition-management centers or somethin', but ain't been nobody takin' care of him for a long time."

Pook's careful eyes scanned the kid. "Axe me, he lookin' sick. Big belly like that can come from not havin' enough food. Like them poor little bruthas an' sistas in Africa."

Dante nodded. "Yeah. An' check out his hair, all nappy an' wild."

"He never talk much," added Pook. "'Cept axin' us for money every day."

Wyatt shrugged again. "So, what else you 'spect him to say? Ain't like he'd have a lot to talk about."

Dante sighed. "Everbody gots a story in Babylon, but nobody gots time to hear 'em. Well, I'ma give him my lunch dollar again. I hate seein' little bruthas an' sistas beggin'."

"Some of 'em only doin' it for rock money, man," said Wyatt.

"Well, duh! But I don't figure he one of them."

"Don't got the symptoms," agreed Pook. "You can always tell by the eyes. His only scared."

Wyatt closed his own eyes. "Well, it your green, Dante. Anyhow, it Wednesday, an' that mean all-you-can-eat meat loaf at my mom's café, so you can spare the change."

Dante frowned. "So? I still give him my dollar anyways.

Yo. My dad say it be like kickin' one more brick out from under Babylon every time we help each other."

Wyatt jerked a thumb toward the kids fighting on the court. "Yeah? An', stupid suckas like them jam *ten* bricks right back in for every one you kick out!"

Dante got to his feet. Pook rose too and reached into his pocket. "Gots me a quarter. I give him that."

Both boys looked down at Wyatt.

The fat boy groaned. "Aw, hell! I just wanna sit here till the bell ring!"

Dante grinned. "Aw, c'mon, man. Kick a brick."

Wyatt sighed, then struggled to his feet and yanked up his shorts. "Okay. I in for a quarter, I guess. Down with Babylon."

The boys headed over to the fence. The kid on the sidewalk waited, fingers still clutching the mesh, looking like a child locked out of a picnic. The kid's clothes were ragged and dirty: a baggy jail jacket of faded blue denim and a grimy T-shirt that might once have been white, above old SilverTabs that looked almost like leather, and ancient Adidas with mismatched laces. A greasy black X cap was clamped backward on a woolly-wild bush of rusty-red hair. There were many mixed children in Oakland, and at first glance this seemed to be one, yet Dante still wondered if this boy could be from some other land. Lots of black people had rust-colored hair, but this kid's just somehow seemed different. His face looked foreign too: broad at the cheekbones but tapering down to a V-shaped chin. His nose was bridgeless but very wide. His mouth was also wide, but his lips just full enough to give it expression. His eyes were set some distance apart in a way that went well with the width of the cheeks. They were large and bronze-toned with a shading of green. The kid's complexion was a beautiful brilliant brown, like fresh cocoa powder, but his lips were a rich ruby red, like pictures of apples in grocery store ads. His face was dirty, the sooty-streaked look that belonged to the homeless, but if you scoped really close you could make out a dusting of freckles over his nose. The small fingers laced in the fence could have been half-sized copies of Dante's own delicate ones, but the kid's fingernails showed crescents of dirt. He looked a young thirteen and still mostly childlike, that age when some boys are almost more pretty than handsome. The big baggy jacket was buttoned even in the afternoon heat and hid most of what might have been a baby-chub body, except for the bulge of a big round tummy. Dante's eyes saddened a little as he flashed the peace sign and offered his dollar.

The boy's fragile brown fingers curled tight on the wrinkled old paper, but his green-tinted eyes met Dante's black ones and saw no mockery there. He accepted the dollar with dignity. His voice had a high, husky squeak as if it wasn't used much. "Thanks."

There were crinkly metal sounds as he shifted position to pocket the bill. Dante saw that the jacket's flap pockets were stuffed with aluminum cans. He exchanged glances with Wyatt, who stepped forward and held out his coin.

"Thanks."

Pook was carefully scanning the kid. He offered his quarter. The kid gave Pook a scope in return, seeming to admire his body, then said thanks once again before turning to go.

Pook's voice was gentle. "Yo."

The kid turned around with a clatter of cans. "Yeah?"

Pook smiled. "That the first time y'all say somethin' 'cept thanks."

The bronze-green eyes searched Pook's as if for a sign. "Sooo . . . what should I say?"

Dante smiled. "You could try tellin' us your name, man." He pointed. "That Wyatt. He Pook. I'm Dante."

The kid met the other boys' eyes, seeming more shy than suspicious. "Well, I'm Radgi. Thanks for the money."

"Kick a minute, man," said Pook as the kid turned to leave once more. "You cool, brutha? What I axin' is, y'all ain't sick or somethin'?"

". . . I'm okay." A mix of expressions crossed the kid's face, the last a small smile. "Are you? I've never seen you playin' any games."

Pook shrugged. "I kinda got me a handicap."

The kid studied Pook's body again. "What?"

"He gender-challenged," snickered Wyatt.

"Huh?"

Wyatt glanced at Pook. "Y'all gonna say the G-word, or should I?"

Pook made a face. "I gay, man."

The kid's eyes went wide in wonder. *"You?* You sure don't look like it!" He hesitated a moment, then added, "Um, does anybody else know?"

Pook grinned. "Everbody know, even it ain't nobody's business."

A flash of understanding seemed to pass between Radgi and Pook. Radgi smiled. "Now I know why you're always out here instead of playing with the other boys."

"He'd *like* to play with the other boys," said Wyatt.

Pook snorted. "Oh, shut up. I got values."

Wyatt grinned and slapped his belly. "Don't take much to figure why *I* always out here, huh?"

Radgi smiled again. "I think you're kinda cool. You aren't somebody a little kid would be scared of."

"I dunno," muttered Pook. "He might want to eat 'em."

Wyatt punched his shoulder. "Oh, shut up, or I might make believe you a cupcake, pony-boy."

Then, Dante felt Radgi scanning his own midnight body. He'd never given much thought about how he looked, but the interest in Radgi's eyes now sparked a sensation of pride. It was stupid, but he suddenly wanted to puff his small chest.

"Um?" asked Radgi. "Are you gay too?"

Dante tried not to frown. "No. There somethin' wrong with my heart. My mom was on crack when she had me. . . . She died."

". . . Oh. I'm sorry."

"So," said Pook. "What wrong with you, Radgi?" He aimed a finger at the kid's jutting stomach. "Y'all gettin' enough to eat?"

Radgi glanced down and frowned. "Sure."

"Well, y'all ever been checked by a doctor? You could have worms."

"*Worms!*" Radgi drew back a pace. "No! I'm just a little chubby, that's all. Like Wyatt."

Wyatt smiled. "That the flyest thing anybody ever said 'bout me."

Dante moved against the fence, raising his arms and gripping the mesh. "Yo, Radgi. It cool. Pook here gonna be a doctor. He always axin' stuff like that."

". . . Oh." Radgi's eyes returned to Pook. "You know about doctor things?"

"Oh sure . . . well, a little. I got me a medical book."

"Aw, he totally up on all that," said Wyatt. "Brutha we know got himself shot in a drive-by. Right here in the side, man. Couldn't go to no hospital 'cause the pigs woulda drilled him. Pook took the bullet out with nuthin' but a ice pick an' some tweezers! I even got pictures!"

"Whoa!" said Radgi.

Dante pushed the dreds back to show the gold ring in his ear. "Check this, Radgi. Pook done it for me when he only seven. His first operation! An', he gonna be fixin' my heart in a few more years."

Radgi's eyes turned back to Pook, and Dante felt something like envy. He jammed his hands in his pockets and kicked the toe of his Nike in the dirt. But then Radgi came closer to the fence.

"Those are way cool dreds, Dante. And that's a real pretty necklace too."

"Uh . . . oh, thanks, man. My dad give me that. It be from Jamaica."

"Are you a real Rastafarian?"

"Well, I don't smoke no ganja, but I believe in Jah, an' tryin' to love people, don't matter if they rate it or not."

Suddenly, Pook's head came up, alert, as the skip-firing thunder of a huge V-10 engine bumped rumbling vibrations down the street. Radgi looked uncertain and moved backward against the fence. Dante, Pook, and Wyatt clutched at the mesh like prisoners and stared up the block as a burly black beast on four massive tires cruised toward them.

"Oh, maaan!" Dante sighed. "I in *luuuuve!*"

"Oh, sure," muttered Pook.

Wyatt stared at the oncoming car, so black that it glowed like a hole in the day. "The hell that?"

"Viper," sighed Dante, clinging to the fence like a crucified kid, the mesh pressing X patterns into his chest. "Eight-liter engine, four hundred horses, zero to sixty in four-point-five seconds!"

Wyatt shrugged. "Don't cream your jeans, B. So, how much a ride like that cost?"

"Fifty big bills."

"Oh. Chump change."

Dante frowned. "Porsche almost a hundred!"

"Yeah but you get a *roof.*"

"Oh, shut up!"

"I think the Viper kicks," said Pook.

Wyatt grinned. "Ain't doctors s'posed to want Beamers?"

"Oh, shut up!"

"Well," said Wyatt. "Somebody gots to be makin' it in Babylon, rollin' a ride like that."

Dante's eyes narrowed a little as the car came closer. "Don't take seven to figure how *that* boy get green!"

Pook stretched to his full height, then raised up on tiptoes, squinting into the sunglare reflected from the Viper's metal-sheathed muscle. "Oh, maaan!"

Wyatt turned. "What?"

Pook sank down on the soles of his Cons, his wide shoulders sagging. "I in *luuuuve!*"

Dante poked him in the side. "Oh, suuure!"

"Well, I know he a punk, but he a *beautiful* punk! I got hormones too, y'know?"

"Don't confuse 'em no more'n they already are," muttered Wyatt. He shaded his eyes with his hand as the car slowed and came angling toward the sidewalk. "Aw, shit! Shoulda knowed it be *him!* Really come up since he drop out school last year, huh?"

Dante scowled. "Don't call what he doin' 'comin' up,' fool!"

The Viper eased to a stop at the curb. "Money in the Ghetto," by Too Short, bumped from big speakers. The boy behind the Viper's wheel looked almost a part of the car. Like the machine, he seemed to be sculpted from midnight-black metal. His big shirtless body seemed all solid muscle: heavy-slabbed chest, bulging biceps, and a stomach like ripples of stone. But his proportions were pumped up and awkward from workouts. About eighteen, his ebony face was too hard to be handsome, and his fade too perfect to fit him.

Radgi had gone tense, small hands clenching to little brown fists and crinkling the cans in the jail jacket pockets. "I gotta go now."

The boy in the car killed the engine and hopped over the door to the sidewalk. Two beepers were clipped to his big ganxta jeans, one purple, one pink, and both bright fluorescent. A flip-phone in a black leather holster was slung like an old-time six-shooter on one hip. His new high-top Hoop Dreams landed him silently on the dirty cement.

"Yo! That you, Radgi?"

The kid hesitated, then took a defiant stance. "Yeah, Air Touch, it's me. So what?"

The big boy only grinned and stepped up to Radgi. "Wondered where you got to." He thoughtfully scanned the kid's big round tummy, then shifted his eyes to the pocketsful of cans. "You down with what's up yet?"

Radgi seemed to be shaking a little, as if wanting to leave but frozen by anger or fear. "Kiss my ass!"

Dante sensed Radgi's helpless rage. Grabbing the fence mesh, he rattled it hard. "Leave him alone, Air Touch!"

Air Touch turned toward the fence. "What you all about, bitch?" His gunmetal eyes considered the eight feet of link and barbed wire, then he grinned and stepped close, crossing his arms over his chest. "Well, check it out! Should be some kinda sign sayin' don't feed the monkeys!" He studied Pook for a moment, as if comparing the younger boy's body with his own, then looked back at Dante. "You the crack baby with the bad fuel pump. Careful, boy, y'all might get a vapor lock. 'Specially if somebody do . . . THIS!"

Air Touch whipped back his arm, then slammed the heel of his hand into the fence against Dante's chest. Dante staggered back, falling to his knees, his hands clutching over his heart. His eyes rolled up and he sucked air in gasps.

Pook's body snapped tense as steel. Cursing, he almost leaped up to scale the fence, but then dropped to the dirt beside Dante, his arms going around the other boy's shoulders. "Lay back, man! On the ground! Here, I help you!"

Air Touch laughed, watching Pook lay Dante down. Dante's eyes were squeezed shut and his small chest heaved for breath. Air Touch stepped to the fence, gripping the links and grinning at the boys on the ground.

"Yo, Rastamon! I thought Jah-love s'posed to fix anythin'! An', *you,* faggot-boy! Try kissin' him all better! Best do it quick, 'fore he die of a broken heart!"

The crackle of cans was the only warning. Too late, Air Touch spun around as Radgi slashed out with a box knife. The razor ripped across Air Touch's up-flung forearm. A spurt of bright blood spattered the sidewalk. Air Touch cursed and leaped back, easily dodging the next clumsy slash. His eyes went wide in surprise for a second, then slitted in fury. Blood dripped from his arm, but his lips curled in a smile. His hand dipped into his pocket and came out with a switchblade. The knife was old but looked well made and not some piece of Taiwanese junk. He thumbed the button and the steel snicked out in the sun. He held the knife almost delicately, like a doctor would hold a scalpel when he knew exactly where he was going to cut. He smiled once more as Radgi edged away. "You step to the wrong man, little bitch!"

But then another metallic click sounded, and Wyatt's voice cut steady and strong. "Chill, shithead!"

Air Touch froze. The only movement was his eyes, flicking to find Wyatt gripping a cheap little Chinese pistol with both chubby thumbs cocked on the hammer. The small gun seemed toylike against Wyatt's bulk, but Air Touch lowered his knife. His big pumped-up body seemed to deflate like a slashed truck tire. For a few seconds there was only the sound of Dante's desperate breaths. Then a new expression crossed Air Touch's face; almost curiosity.

"How you get that past the metal detector?"

Wyatt's eyes never wavered, but he lowered one hand to pat his huge hanging mass of belly blubber. "How you think, fool?"

Air Touch's tongue moved over his lips. He tried a smile. "Hey. You all that, bruthaman."

Wyatt snorted. *"Brutha?* My ass! You ain't even the same *species* as us!" Gripping the gun in both hands again, Wyatt aimed square at Air Touch's big chest. "Lose the blade . . . *reptile!* Carefully! Then crawl in your showtime snakemobile an' slither your slimy punk-ass back to the sewer where you come from!"

Heat shimmered up from the sidewalk, but that wasn't why Air Touch was sweating. Eyes on the gun, he folded the knife and eased it back into his pocket. Then he held up both palms and backed cautiously toward the car. Wyatt poked the gun muzzle through the mesh and kept him locked in the sights. "Carefully! I know you gots steel in there, but don't even *think* about it!"

One of Air Touch's beepers went off. He almost jumped out of his skin. Radgi's high-husky voice carried above the pager's squeaky pips.

"Yo, ass-wipe! Maybe it's your mommy callin'! Time to go home for milk an' cookies!"

Air Touch reached to shut it off.

"Carefully, boy," Wyatt reminded.

Sweat streamed down Air Touch's face and gleamed on his muscle-bulked body as he punched the tiny button and the beeping cut off. He slipped a hand behind him to grasp the door handle. His tongue ran over his lips again. "I gotta use my hand, man . . . to turn the key . . . an' shift gears, y'know?"

Wyatt nodded once. *"One* hand, punk! Keep the other one on the wheel! Just like they do on the Bad Cops show!"

Opening the door, Air Touch slowly slid in, but then paused to give Radgi a look. "Nowhere to run, bitch. Remember that!"

The kid just flipped him a fragile brown finger.

A bell jangled back at the school building. On the ground, Dante was struggling to sit up with Pook's help. His breath still came hard, but he managed to gasp, "Hell! We gonna get tardies!"

"Naw," said Pook. "Not if we don't take showers."

Air Touch fired the Viper's engine.

"Carefully house *boy!"* called Wyatt once more. The gun held steady as Air Touch shifted into first and the black car thundered away.

Then, Radgi ran to the fence. "Dante! You okay?"

Dante nodded. "It ain't as bad as it look. It was only a little one."

Wyatt watched the Viper as it retreated down the street, then he glanced across the school yard where the rest of the class was moving toward the gym. "Bell always stop the fights, even if Coach can't. All them fools nuthin' but doggy-dogs droolin' to the game." Grunting, he lifted a handful of blubber and tucked the little gun somewhere beneath, then turned to Radgi. "Yo, man!

What you done, that took balls! Nobody step to Air Touch before! Wish I had my camera!"

Dante got to his feet with Pook's help. "You cool, Radgi?"

Radgi met Dante's eyes for a moment. Dante wasn't sure what the look carried, concern or sympathy. He suddenly realized that he'd been seeing that look for most of his life. It stirred something inside him now, something almost like anger that a homeless hood-rat might be feeling sorry for him.

"Yeah," said Radgi. "I'm okay. Um, maybe I'll see you brothers around? Carefully, Dante."

Dante turned away, now feeling ashamed that it took so little to put him out of the game. "Yeah. Carefully, Radgi."

Wyatt took Dante's arm. "C'mon! Don't need no detention!"

Dante shook free of Wyatt's hand. "I can walk by myself!"

They headed off across the dusty playing field. Pook glanced over his shoulder toward the fence. "I still say I seen Radgi someplace before."

A few minutes later they reached the gym's locker-room door. Dante's breathing was still a little ragged, and he propped himself against the brick wall. Other boys were coming out, most dressed in big jeans and T-shirts and smelling like school soap or underarm sprays. Some carried backpacks slung on their shoulders. A swampy mix of shower steam and sweat drifted in the afternoon air, mingled with the young-male scents of wet towels and old jockstraps and socks.

"Pook," said Wyatt. "Slide in an' snag our stuff. Nobody wanna shower with you anyways."

Pook made a face, but slipped through the doorway. Two other boys coming out exchanged uneasy glances and moved quickly apart to let him pass. Dante rested the back of his head against the wall.

"Yo, Wyatt, I think you was right, 'bout Radgi bein' from somewheres else. He talk different."

Wyatt nodded. "He talk like he raised somewhere better."

"Wonder what happen to his parents?"

"Prob'ly got eaten."

"Huh?"

Wyatt pointed toward the peeling Victorian houses and grimy brick buildings surrounding the school. "Babylon eat up a lotta people, man. Just like your dad always sayin'."

Dante sighed. "Babylon eat its own young, what my dad say." Then he frowned and stood up straight. "You got to be strong or you just another victim in this place. Strong an' cool an' down with the flava."

Wyatt smiled. "Or smart enough to stay out of the game."

Dante shook his head. "Bullets don't care if you a player or not. Or how smart you are. Or how good. Or who you want to be when you grow up. Bullets don't give you no choice."

Pook emerged from the locker room with two backpacks slung by their straps on one shoulder. The boys quickly dressed, Dante and Pook pulling baggy Rye jeans over their gym shorts, while Wyatt stuffed himself into Big Smith dungarees that he couldn't button all the way. Dante tugged on a well-worn tan T-shirt with sleeves that had shrunk and rode high on his arms. Wyatt's black tee was a souvenir from the Oakland Zoo that showed a sleepy-looking lion. It stretched skintight on his roly-poly chest, and his belly hung out underneath while brown bulges of blubber spilled over his jeans on each side. Pook's shirt was a tight white tank top that clung to his pecs like a coat of paint. Wyatt gave him a glance.

"Don't know who you jockin' for, man. You the only one of your kind around here."

Pook smiled and shrugged. "Like, I gots a choice?" He shouldered his own purple pack, then picked up Dante's red one. "I carry it for ya."

Dante grabbed it. "I can carry my own!"

The boys started for the school building.

"Hey, homo!"

Pook came to a stop, his body tensed and his strong hands curled to fists. "Ooooo . . . SHIT! Don't it never stop!"

The boys swung around as three others came trotting toward them. All were seniors from the football team, the biggest a yellow-brown boy who massed even more than Air Touch. All wore shorts and mesh jerseys to show buff. The first boy yanked a bill from his pocket and fluttered it in his fingers. "Yo, bitch! Here's a Jackson to do me like Michael!"

The other big G's stood flexed, their looks warning Dante and Wyatt to chill. Wyatt's hand slipped beneath his belly for the gun, but Pook was free of his pack in a second. Almost before it hit the ground, his arm shot out like a bronze lightning bolt. His fist slammed into the first boy's jaw with the sound of somebody chopping raw meat. The boy's head snapped back and he crashed to the pavement. One of the other boys leaped forward and Pook kicked him almost casually in the crotch. The boy doubled over and puked, then fell to his knees in the mess. The last boy stepped back, spreading his palms, and stood staring. Wyatt took his hand out from under his stomach and gave him a shrug.

"Wemarkabo, huh?"

Pook stood, looking down at the first boy, his feet wide apart and his hands half-curled on slim hips. The boy struggled up on his elbows, shaking his head slowly, his eyes looking glassy and lost. Pook leaned forward and snagged the twenty from between his fingers.

"Y'all just got done, sucka! Be sure an' tell everybody how a homo put you on your back!"

"Yeah!" added Wyatt. "Don't ya hate it when that happen?"

Pocketing the bill, Pook shouldered his pack once more. Dante gazed at Pook for a moment, wondering why he didn't seem proud of taking those big busters down, but then turned and walked away. Pook and Wyatt followed, leaving the other boys moaning and cursing behind. Pook frowned, then winced a little as he massaged his fist with his other hand. "I get so sick of that bullshit!"

Wyatt glanced over his shoulder to where the first boy was struggling to his feet, helped by the third, while the second lay curled and groaning on the ground. "Guess he caught you at the wrong time of the month, huh? Wish I had my camera."

"Oh, shut up."

All three stories of school windows were open. The back entrance doors yawned wide on their stops, yet the air wafting out seemed even hotter than the asphalt courtyard. There were scents of old wood and floor wax, of well-worn sport shoes and hair sheen, and natural kid-sweat that all the perfume in the world couldn't cover. The halls were too crowded with kids changing classes to echo, and the hundreds of voices combined in a single-note roar like the rhythm of hard winter rain on a roof. The boys battled their way to the stairwell against everyone fighting to get somewhere else before the bell rang again. Dante and Pook moved in a wedge behind Wyatt, who plowed steadily on like a bulldozer padded in blubber. Teachers called to each other and occasionally cursed, but stayed in the safety of classroom door-ways. Pook nudged Dante and pointed with a grin as they passed room 34: Mr. Elroy, the algebra teacher, was pouring a Jack Daniel's miniature into his big coffee mug. Dante smiled slightly, then suddenly stared up as he reached the foot of the stairs. Wyatt started to climb, swearing as always when faced with a staircase, but Dante stepped back against the banister.

"Aw, hell. My shirt be on backward!"

"Huh?" Pook stopped as Dante stripped off his tee and turned it over in his hands. Pook cocked his head, then sucked in his cheeks to cover a grin as two eighth-grade girls squeezed past Wyatt and came down the steps. Dante glanced up as if surprised, still turning his T-shirt inside out. "Yo! Hi, Shara."

Both girls paused and exchanged secret glances. The one called Shara was as velvety black as Dante, her full-figured form clad in Levi's Loose Fits and a Deep Threadz half-tee that showed off a soft puppy-tummy. Her breasts swung heavy and free, and, standing below, Dante could see their round shapes as she descended the stairs. Heat spread through his loins.

Shara's hair was cut close, and the style went fly with her natural pout and the baby-chub padding her features. One tube in the overhead fluorescent was flickering, and Dante wasn't sure if it was just a reflection or really a small spark of interest that lit Shara's eyes as they met his a second before slipping down over his bare-chested body. The light buzzed and dimmed. Had that been a smile on her lips, he wondered, or only a shadow?

Then, Shara stepped past him and there was no doubting the smile she gave Pook. He smiled in return, looking way too male. Dante yanked his shirt back on, frowning as Shara touched Pook's hand.

"How you hurt your knuckles like that, Pooky?"

Pook shrugged, handsome and cool. "Ain't nuthin'."

Wyatt had stopped six steps above. "Trajectory of his fist intersect the orbit of some sucka's face!" he called down.

Shara took Pook's hand in her own, delicate midnight clasping hard bronze. "Y'all best take care, Pooky. Doctor can't go messin' up his hands."

Bells rang on three floors. Kids cursed and swore and put on more speed to reach the last class of the day. Shara let go of Pook's hand. "Carefully, boy."

"Oh, sure. Bye, Shara."

"C'mon, *Pooky!*" yelled Wyatt. "We gonna get tardies!"

Shara moved down the hall with her friend, but paused to look over her shoulder. "Bye, Dante."

". . . Uh. Oh. Bye, Shara."

Wyatt had made it to the second floor. Sweat shone on his

forehead and darkened the T-shirt under his arms. "Come ON! An', don't you go gettin' another one of your 'tacks, Dante! Nobody got time for it!"

Dante started up the steps. Pook climbed beside him and took his arm, but Dante shook off his hand. "I cool, damnit!"

"How come you say your shirt backward, Dante?"

"Cause it was!"

"No it wasn't."

"Yes it was, stupid!"

Pook shrugged. "Okay, it was. But, now it really is."

Dante glanced down. "Ooooo, HELL!" Ripping his shirt off once more, he whipped it the right way around and yanked it back on. "Damnit, Pook, you don't even *like* girls!"

"Oh, sure I do, Dante. I like 'em just fine."

Dante reached the top of the stairs, panting. *"What?"*

"Oh, sure. Girls are cool, man. It like I don't gotta front for 'em. They know who I am, an' all that."

"Hell, you don't front for nobody, Pook."

"Sure I do. Sometimes. Like, when we uptown or in a other hood. Them times when it hard enough just bein' black."

Dante stared at Pook. ". . . Oh. I never knew that."

Pook smiled. "Anyway, Shara was really talkin' to you."

"She . . . was?"

"Oh, sure. Girls be like that, man. Come at ya at a angle." Pook's smile widened to a grin. "Shara like what you done with your shirt, but it just wasn't the right time for lettin' you know she like it."

". . . Oh. Um, you really think so?"

"Oh, sure."

Wyatt had stopped halfway down the hall. He pointed to the only classroom door still standing open. *"C'mon,* damnit!"

A boy was leaning against the lockers near the doorway. He was smoking a Kool and coming casual about it while keeping an eye out for the enemy. Korean, he was about fourteen, his face round and friendly, his almond eyes bright above chub-cushioned cheeks. His hair was a shaggy black mop that covered his ears and shaded his eyes, and his body was gold-brown and barrel-shaped in a red Top Dawg T-shirt and OshKosh overalls. He grinned and flashed peace as the other three boys came trotting down the hall.

"No hurry, kids. Miz Tyehimba late. Yo, Dante, put it in park 'fore you get an attack."

Dante slowed to a walk, then stopped by the door. Bending over, he gripped his knees with his hands and sucked a few breaths with his head lowered. As if to confirm that the teacher was late, a paper plane sailed out the doorway and laughter followed its flight. Dante straightened, then pointed to the Korean boy's Kool.

"Yo, Kelly, can I have a hit?"

Kelly cocked his head, but shrugged. "Sure, kid."

Pook frowned as Dante took the cigarette and sucked deep. "Y'all shouldn't be doin' that, Dante."

Dante let smoke out slow. "The hell! I can't do *nuthin'*, man! Just like Coach say, what choices I got?"

Kelly spread his hands. "Y'all shouldn't be listenin' to that ole wack, kid. He all the time raggin' on me to join his karate team. The hell I know 'bout karate?"

Wyatt leaned against the lockers and wiped sweat from his forehead. "Yo, Dante. You wanna come G, why didn't you axe Air Touch for some of his smoke? The first one always free."

Dante scowled and passed the cigarette back, ignoring the fat boy. "So, Kelly? You on Coach's loser list, too?"

"Yeah. He got me an' Jinx walkin' laps every day in fourth period. Thought about tryin' for a transfer so I could hang with you kids, but it too late in the year."

"Um, let me cap the Kool, okay?"

Kelly shrugged again. "Your funeral, kid." He passed

Dante the smoke, then scoped the empty hallway. "Yo, Wyatt. Got two cans, Krylon. The real dope. You up?"

Wyatt looked thoughtful. "Mmm. Maybe. What colors?"

"Gloss black an' chrome silver. Straight-up O-Town colors."

"Well, I still got 'bout a half can of black left. What I really be needin' is Chevrolet red, but I might take the silver. How much?"

"For you? List."

Wyatt smiled. "*Your* list, what you sayin'."

"Well, hell, Wyatt, green the only color I need. An', where else y'all gonna score genuine Kry? *With* nozzles."

"Mmm. So, where it live?"

"In my locker. Yo, Pook, Dante. Do the watch, huh?"

Dante let smoke trickle casually from his nose. "Sure, kid." Pook nodded and turned toward the stairwell to listen for anyone coming up from the ground floor or down from the third. He glanced back with a frown as Dante sucked smoke again.

"Now, what you all about, fool?"

Dante gazed at the smoldering cigarette. "Maybe I just wanna live a little 'fore I die."

Pook considered that. "Well, I know what you sayin', Dante. But, you gotta be thinkin' ahead."

Dante sighed, sucking the last hit from the Kool before flipping it away. "Why? That ass-wipe Air Touch coulda capped us all today, man. Right out there in the *school yard*, an' none of us even playin' the game! All the 'thinkin' ahead' in the world don't buy you no choices in Babylon!"

He turned to watch as Kelly opened his locker and pulled out two cans of spray paint. Wyatt took one and weighed it expertly on his palm, then popped off the cap.

"Check it," said Kelly. "Still cherry."

"Well, don't bug or nuthin', but I seen that number before." Wyatt pulled the nozzle free and inspected it carefully. "Look like you right, man. I take this silver. Can I owe ya till Friday?"

"*You?* Go without sayin', kid. Take the black too. You can have both for my cost, plus twenty."

Wyatt replaced the nozzle and cap. "Okay. But, figure you score me a red?"

Kelly nodded. "You got it, kid. Next week."

Pook came alert. "Miz Tyehimba on her way up!"

Kelly closed his locker, and Wyatt came back with the cans. "Here, Dante, stash 'em in your pack. We got enough for a hit now. Beautify Babylon."

The boys entered the classroom. Kelly flashed a sign, clueing the kids that the teacher was coming. The noise level dropped slightly. A couple of blunts were pinched out and put by for later, and a few cigarettes were casually flipped through the wide-open windows. Smoke still drifted near the ceiling, an eye-burning mix of tobacco and ganja, but Mrs. Tyehimba had taught at this school too many years to be bothered by that. Wyatt squeezed into his desk in the last row. Dante, Pook, and Kelly took their places in the row in front of him. Pook sat to Dante's right. Beside Dante on the left was a sad-looking boy in a ragged mesh T-shirt. He might once have been chubby, but now his body looked more like soot-colored pudding slopped over bone. He had flabby little breasts instead of a chest, and his stomach flopped over old Chinese jeans that Kelly had given him six months ago and which probably hadn't been washed since. His face was pear-shaped and pudgy, wide-nosed with loose lips, and his mouth hung perpetually open to show big buck teeth, one chipped. He slumped in his seat with his chin in his hands and sucked on a licorice stick. Dante leaned close and nudged him with his elbow. "Yo, Jinx. Can I have one?"

"Zuh? Oh . . . sure." Jinx reached into a little paper sack and handed Dante a stick. His dull black eyes drifted to the door as Mrs. Tyehimba came in. "She just make ya toss it, man."

Dante smiled and slipped the licorice into his mouth like a long black cigar. "Bet?"

Jinx only shrugged and dropped his chin back into his hands.

Mrs. Tyehimba usually wore an expression somewhere between hope and despair. It didn't change much as she walked to the front of the room and took roll with a sweep of experienced eyes. She'd faced down a few guns and knives in her day, and most of her students left history class knowing at least a little more about the world than when they came in.

Dante supposed that he liked her . . . as much as you *could* like a teacher, anyway. He usually maintained a *B* average in history. Wyatt did the same, and Pook always got *A* 's and *B* 's in everything but PE.

Mrs. Tyehimba explained that a teacher's meeting had made her late, and complimented the class for not throwing their desks out the windows . . . or something like that . . . while they were waiting. Then, Dante felt her wire-guided eyes lock on target.

"Dante. You know that Jinx is the only student allowed to have licorice in class."

A few kids snickered. Some turned in their seats to give Dante sly grins, but he just kept the stick in his mouth, talking around it.

"I need it too, Miz Tyehimba. I'ma bring you my note tomorrow."

Nothing much ever surprised Mrs. Tyehimba, so Dante enjoyed her shocked look all the more. Murmurs rippled the now quiet room. Even Jinx seemed amazed. Kelly cocked an eyebrow, Pook just sucked in his cheeks, and Wyatt rolled his eyes toward the ceiling and muttered about wishing for his camera.

Dante's eyes cruised around, checking reactions. Most of the class was staring at him. A few faces showed only disgust, but more looked surprised and some even sad. The two dope smokers exchanged I-told-ya-so glances. One boy near the chalkboard looked pissed, but that was because he figured he'd just lost a customer he never knew he'd had.

Mrs. Tyehimba cleared her throat to cover whatever she felt.

"I'm glad to see you fighting your addiction, Dante. I know we all wish you courage." Then she turned to the board. "Open your books to page 257. The sweeping changes in South Africa have made most of this chapter obsolete."

Book pages rustled like leaves in the wind. The dealer-boy flipped Dante off. Kelly leaned past Pook to give Dante a whatt-up look for a second. Jinx nudged Dante and offered another licorice stick.

"Here, brutha. Uh, wanna come with me to rehab after school? It better when you got friends to help you self-inciner-ate."

"Huh?" Dante took the licorice, but had trouble meeting the other boy's sympathetic eyes. "Um . . . no thanks, man. I . . . gotta fight this alone, what it is."

Jinx's chin quivered a moment, but he clamped his teeth hard on the licorice. Then he sighed. "I try that. But, I here for ya, brutha."

Pook's elbow jabbed Dante's ribs. "Shut up, fool!"

"Yeah!" hissed Wyatt. "We gonna talk after school, wack-ass! Believe it!"

"Oh, all you go to hell!" Dante hissed back.

Mrs. Tyehimba turned from the chalkboard. "Dante. Would you share with the class your opinions on the recent events in South Africa?"

Dante felt blood rush to his face. "I . . . don't got no opinions 'bout nuthin' . . . an', an' nobody care if I did."

Snickers ran around the room. The teacher frowned. "Surely you have some interest in the future of Africa?"

Dante glared. "Why I care 'bout what happen in Africa? Ain't my home no more!" He jumped to his feet and stabbed a finger toward the windows. "That be *my* future out there . . . no choice in hell, an' prob'ly gettin' my ass capped by my very own people! Shit! We all just little black ants in Babylon, waitin' to get stepped on an' too stupid to see it!"

Stunned silence settled. Faces stared at Dante, some open-mouthed. Only Wyatt murmured, "Wemarkabo." For the second time in history, Mrs. Tyehimba looked genuinely shocked.

"Dante, I realize that withdrawal is hard. Maybe you should go out into the hall until you calm down."

"Life is hard," muttered Dante, stalking from the room. "Then you get stepped on!"

"The hell wrong with you, Dante?" demanded Pook as the three boys came down the school steps and into the glaring afternoon sun.

"Yeah!" said Wyatt, descending slowly because he couldn't see his feet. "What all this buggin' about? Only reason you didn't get detention for the rest of the year 'cause Miz Tyehimba figure you stressed from comin' off crack!"

Pook touched Dante's shoulder. "Yeah. An', why you figure it cool to come frontin' crackhead?"

Dante yanked at his pack straps. Wyatt's spray cans clattered together inside. "Both you fools get the hell out my face!"

Wyatt gave Dante a shove. Dante stumbled and cursed, almost falling, then spun back around and cocked a fist. "Do that again, I'ma kick your ass, boy!"

Wyatt stopped, just grinning and patting his stomach. "Hit me, y'all never find your fist again, Buster Brown."

"Awwww, *hell!*" Dante turned back around and started for the gates. Pook caught up in a few easy strides and grabbed his shoulder.

"Yo! Like Wyatt say in class, we gonna talk, man. Come correct an' quit spittin' G like you all that!"

"Leave me alone, sucka!" Jerking free of Pook's grip, Dante spun around once more and ripped off his pack, letting it drop to the concrete. He spread his feet, his small chest heaving beneath his T-shirt. "Just leave me the hell alone!"

Pook offered open palms. "Chill, Dante. Be cool."

Dante's voice broke. *"Cool?* The hell *you* know 'bout bein' cool, you . . . you big joke!"

Other kids parted to pass them. Some snickered and grinned. "Go for it, Dante!" one called. "Yeah!" urged another. "Put the bitch on his back!"

A familiar circle was starting to form. Dante had seen thousands of them, but this was the first time he'd been in the middle. The feeling was intense; new, and not exactly scary like he'd always thought it would be. All eyes were on him, most expectant, some skeptical, but none showing sympathy. Wyatt stood back, looking more disgusted than anything else. Dante's gaze flicked past Pook to the security guard in the school building doorway. The man looked tired and hot, and probably figured he'd already done his job for the day. He turned his back and started to mess with the metal detector. The circle of kids was closing in tighter. Some shouted curses and taunts to get things goin' on. Dante was surprised at how many seemed to be on his side, and yet he felt strangely alone. Other kids hurried past, wanting to watch but afraid of missing their bus. The yelling and shouts echoed in Dante's ears, yet seemed strangely distant. His vision seemed to narrow until he and Pook were the only clear shapes. He knew what was coming: Already his chest felt like some huge weight was crushing it in. His heart began skipping beats like a diesel with dirty injectors. Shadows seemed to hover at the edges of his eyes. This was going to be a bad one . . . the kind the doctors had warned him about. It was funny how they could describe the physical feeling but never the terrible fear. It was like having your mind squeezed out of your skull while a truck ran over your body. And then there would be nothing but a horrible empty loneliness, as if his spirit was wandering lost, searching for something but having no home to come back to. Years ago he'd asked one of the doctors if he died each time this happened. The white man had only glanced at his watch, tossed Dante's file on the desk and picked up another, and said not to worry because all little boys had nine lives, like cats. Dante had counted the times after that and was now up to seven. The only advice the doctors had given was to get somewhere "safe" and use his last breath to cry out for help. Safe? There was nowhere safe in Babylon! His eyes searched the circle of faces, seeing no one he knew except Wyatt and Pook . . . *and how could he ask them to help him, now?*

There wasn't much time! For an instant, he thought he saw a familiar face outside the fence. But, no, it was only Radgi . . . a homeless hood-rat who had no choices either. Then he saw Shara. He couldn't read her expression, yet he felt trapped because there was no way he could get himself out of this sucker's game now and still prove his maleness to her.

He lunged, swinging wild. Pook made no move to dodge. Dante's fist caught him full on the jaw. Pook spit blood and stumbled back, his hands only half-clenched. Dante followed, swinging desperately, feeling his fists go numb as Pook fell. Then his sight flickered and blurred like a worn-out videotape. There wasn't enough air left in the world to fill his struggling lungs. His knees gave and he crumpled to the concrete, glimpsing Pook on the ground among cigarette butts and splotches of gum. Somebody spit. Dante heard Wyatt roar a curse. The last thing he saw was the fat kid flinging some other boy down. The last thing he felt was the side of his face slamming hot sidewalk.

"He's comin' around."

"What go round always does," Dante heard himself mumble. Then he recognized the school nurse's voice. The blackness began to brighten as if he were rising from deep in the sea. He felt a cool cloth on his forehead. He opened his eyes, blinking in the icy white glow of a ceiling fluorescent. The nurse was a big, brawny woman, but there was concern and relief on her face as she bent over Dante, who lay on his back on a cot.

"Hang on, son. The ambulance comin'."

Dante sighed, almost enjoying the feel of soft linen under his body. It took a moment for the nurse's words to register, then he tried to sit up. "Ambulance, hell!"

Startled, the nurse held him down. "Easy, son. Is there somethin' I should be doin'?"

Dante flexed his fingers, feeling the circulation coming back . . . and pain along with it. How had he hurt his hand? "Yeah! Cancel that goddamn ambulance!"

"*Easy*, son," the nurse soothed. "Is there somethin' you need?"

"Yeah. Get me a beer."

"*What?*"

Another voice chuckled, "Oh, sure, Miz Buford. Doctor's orders."

Dante raised up on his elbows, staring at the white canvas curtain beside his cot. There were three beds in the nurse's office, but for logical reasons each was screened off to keep their occupants from seeing one another before cops or paramedics arrived.

"Pook!"

"Welcome back to Babylon, boy."

Mrs. Buford tensed and put a palm on Dante's chest as a hard bronze hand took hold of the curtain and slid it back on its overhead track. Dante rolled on his side to see Pook sitting on the next cot, holding a cotton ball to his nose, its whiteness spotted with blood. Dante's eyes met Pook's a second, shied away in uncertainty, but returned again. "I . . . sorry, man."

Pook shrugged a muscled shoulder. "Oh, sure." He took the cotton off his nose and turned to the nurse. "Yo. This stuff sterile? It smell more like somethin' come out a proctology lab!"

Mrs. Buford scowled. "You watch your mouth, boy!"

Dante grinned. "Sooo, what about my beer?"

"Only thing you gettin' is a ride to the hospital!"

Dante sat up, pushing away the nurse's big arm. "No I ain't, damnit! You figure that free? They charge my dad for it! Fifteen hundred dollars the last time this happen! He still payin' them 'stallments!"

"You lay your butt back down there, boy!"

"Yo! Don't get me pissed! I'ma have me another attack!"

The security guard stood in the doorway with his arms crossed. He was a big man who usually smiled and never fronted as a cop. He chuckled. "Maybe y'all just best give the boy a beer, Gertha. One of them you got stashed in the ice-pack cooler."

"Don't you start, Lionel! You been doin' your job, we both of us be on our way home right now 'stead of wet-nursin' some little ole smarty-mouth fools!"

Dante glared. "Call me no fool, you ole cow!"

Another voice snickered. "Too bad this ain't India, she be sacred."

Both Dante and Pook turned toward the door. Wyatt stood behind the guard. He cocked his head as a siren screamed somewhere in the distance, coming closer.

Dante glanced at Pook, then swung his legs to the floor. The nurse moved to stop him, but then paused and looked uncertain.

"Go for it," said Dante. "Wrestlin' with you be *real* good for my heart!"

Mrs. Buford made an exasperated noise and dropped her hands to her hips before swinging around to scowl at the guard. "Well, what we gonna do 'bout that ambulance now? Them new regulations mean we gonna have five hundred forms need fillin' out!"

Wyatt butted his bulk past the guard and pointed to the third cot, where a pair of Air Jordans showed at the edge of the curtain. "Yo! What about Buster Brown over there?"

The nurse scowled again. "You like to crack his ribs, jumpin' on him!"

"Well, he spit on my homey!"

Dante turned to Pook. "Hell! I sorry, man!"

Pook just smiled. "Oh, sure." He turned to the other curtain. "Yo, mark-ass, it hurt to breathe?"

An angry moan sounded behind the screen. "You goddamn homo! Faggot! Fairy! Queer!"

"Mmm," said Pook. "An' you kiss yo *mama* with a mouth like that?" He grinned at the nurse. "Sure *sound* like busted ribs to me, Miz Buford. Oughta least go in for observation."

Mrs. Buford exchanged glances with Lionel, who coughed to cover a smile. Dante stood and pulled his pack from under the cot.

"C'mon, Pook. Let's bail this Babylonian butt-head factory!"

Pook touched a fingertip to his nose, then flipped the bloody cotton casually into a wastebasket halfway across the room. "Oh, sure."

Wyatt turned to leave, but Mrs. Tyehimba appeared behind the guard. "Wait a minute, boys. Gertha? May I see you a moment?"

Pook picked up his own pack and stepped close to Dante. "Oh, shit!" he whispered as the nurse went into the hall and the guard stepped back to block the doorway. "Now your ass in traction for sure!"

Dante shrugged. "Oh, leave me alone."

Wyatt glanced at Pook and rolled his eyes. *"Déjà vu."*

Somewhere in the street the ambulance siren came screaming up and then blipped into silence. A second later came Mrs. Buford's bellow, "THAT LITTLE FOOL!"

Pook gave Dante a nudge. "What I say?"

Mrs. Buford burst back into the room, shoving the guard aside. Her face was ruddy, and the furious glare she shot Dante could have peeled paint off the walls.

"You little fool! Heart like yours, an' suckin' that garbage! I slap the crap out you, boy . . . I wasn't scared of you dyin' right here! . . . FOOL!" Marching to her desk, she tore open a drawer and flung a small paper bag at Dante. "There somethin' to suck on, fool!" She whomped down in her swivel chair and whipped out her arm as if clearing the air of nasty little things. "Get your black asses out of here! All of you! . . . FOOL!"

"Wish I had my camera," muttered Wyatt.

Dante's eyes trailed the floor, avoiding the stares of the guard and Mrs. Tyehimba as he walked into the hall with Wyatt and Pook behind. The boys stepped aside as two white men came running, rolling a gurney.

"Where's the nurse's office?" one demanded.

Pook pointed. "Right there. Patient be needin' a occipital enema out the starboard ear hole. His brain all blocked up by Babylonian bullshit."

"*What?*"

"Come on," muttered the other. "It's either an OD or gunshot wound."

Pook led the way out the front doors and down the steps. "Fool," he murmured.

"The white guy?" asked Dante.

"You."

". . . Oh. Sorry."

"Oh, sure. That make me feel one whooole lot better."

Wyatt muttered, "Now we gotta wait for the next damn bus!"

Dante spread his hands. "I SORRY! Okay?"

"If you was really sorry, you do somethin' 'bout it."

"Like, what?"

"Like the dishes."

Dante sighed. "Okay."

The boys came out through the school gates and turned to walk down to the corner bus stop. A metal sign on a lamppost read DRUG FREE ZONE, ONE STRIKE YOU'RE OUT. It was pocked by bullets and layered with spray paint. A small figure stood in the sign's patch of shade. A little brown hand flashed two fingers of peace. Dante felt a new sense of comfort as Radgi came to him with a crinkling of cans. The jail jacket was unbuttoned in the heat, and

Dante noticed a clubbiness to Radgi's chest beneath the grimy T-shirt ballooning out over the kid's big tummy. Dante decided that, homeless or not, Radgi had enough of something goin' on to be able to eat. He wondered a moment if the kid had once worked for Air Touch. That idea seemed backed by what had happened outside the school fence, because Air Touch had known his name. Still, it was funny that Dante couldn't really picture this kid selling crack; there seemed to be too much empathy in Radgi's eyes.

"You okay, Dante? I saw what happened. Was it some kind of attack because of your heart?"

Dante nodded. "Yeah. But, like I said, they look a lot worse'n they really are."

"Oh, *sure*," said Pook.

Radgi seemed uncertain. "Well, it *looked* like it really hurt. But, why were you fightin' your homey?"

Pook smiled. "We be Babylon's little black ants."

Radgi turned to Pook. "Um, are you still gonna fix Dante's heart?"

"Oh, sure. What a little blood between bruthas?"

Dante smiled too, then offered the paper bag to Radgi. "Here, man. Want some licorice?"

"Well, I don't *need* it, but, if you don't want it . . ."

"Chill," said Wyatt, grabbing Dante's wrist. "*You* gonna need it for class tomorrow!"

"Yeah," added Pook. "Fool."

"What you sayin'?" Dante demanded.

Pook gave Wyatt a shrug. "Don't got a clue, do he?" Then he faced Dante. "Yo, stupid. Jinx just barely makin' it. Ain't bad enough he hurtin', but now you gotta go an' crack on his rehab like some kinda joke!"

"Oh, hell! I never even thought about that!"

Wyatt shook his head. "'Course you didn't, fool! Ain't nuthin' a *real* G-boy in the game would think about."

"Um," said Radgi. "I know Jinx. He used to buy from Air Touch, but he's tryin' to get clean." Radgi's eyes went to Dante. "Jinx is a good brutha, Dante."

Dante sighed. "I never say he wasn't. Hell, I don't hardly even know him."

"So why are you makin' jokes about his rehab?"

"Damnit, I ain't!" Dante searched three pairs of eyes, then spread his hands. "Sooo, what should I do now?"

"Listen up," said Wyatt. "Word already goin' round you a crackhead. Be all over school by tomorrow. Y'all wanted to get noticed, guess you did . . . fool."

"But, what good it gonna do Jinx?"

"Well," said Pook. "Jinx got no homeys 'cause he come here already addicted. Brutha need friends, what I sayin'."

"Well . . . yeah. But, what can I do 'bout that?"

"Be one," said Wyatt. "Cruise over to rehab with him after school tomorrow."

"Huh? You sayin' to come like I really been on crack? But, that lyin'! An', anyways, how that gonna help him?"

Pook smiled. "What it is, let him figure he helpin' *you.*"

"Yeah," added Wyatt. "Nobody believe what really wrong with you anyways, man; you look too normal. So, nobody got a prob figurin' you been on crack all this time."

"An', Jinx have us for friends," Pook finished.

"Mmm," said Dante. "But, s'pose he don't wanna hang with us?"

Wyatt shrugged. "Then it ain't your prob no more. Each one teach one, an' you tried. Know what I sayin'?"

"An', why you trippin'?" added Pook. "Y'all scared if Jinx come correct, he ain't gonna like you?"

Wyatt grinned. "Yo, Pook! You figure if Dante was a 'normal' B, *he* choose hangin' with losers like us?"

Dante frowned. "Give me that, man! I knowed you bruthas all my life! That make us homeys!"

Radgi had been listening, and now said quietly, "They're right, Dante. It's hard to make friends when you don't have any choices."

Dante studied the smaller kid. It was funny, but he wanted to be friends with Radgi, even though he knew nothing about him.

Wyatt pointed. "Yo! Here the bus. C'mon."

Dante moved to follow the others, but paused and turned back to Radgi. "See you tomorrow, man? Out by the fence? I bring you another dollar."

Radgi smiled. "Sure, Dante. Thanks."

Dante yanked at his pack straps and headed for the bus. He wondered again why having Radgi like him seemed so important. He supposed that he did owe something to Jinx, but what did the friendship of a dirty little hood-rat count for in Babylon?

3

The waterfront side of Dante's home street was blocks of shipping containers stacked six levels high. Huge cranes cruised the rows on legs eighty feet tall, looking like mechanical monsters from space guarding their great piles of eggs while carrying off or adding a few now and then. Container trucks rumbled along the street, some straining with exhaust pipes pouring smoke as they took away eggs to be hatched somewhere while others returned at an easier pace with empty shells that rattled and boomed as they bounced over cracks in the pavement. Dante sometimes wondered who in Babylon got to open those treasure-filled eggs from far-away lands. None were ever hatched in his neighborhood.

The other side of the street was mostly old buildings of rusty sheet metal or crumbling brick where trucks were repaired, sold, or painted. Two ancient Victorian houses remained on one corner like leftover relics from an earlier age. Standing together as if for support, both were a narrow three stories tall with peeling white paint over wood weathered gray. The upper windows of one stared blank and empty, but the ground floor was a little restaurant. The faded sign over its door read AMERICAN CAFE in both English and Chinese, and Wyatt's mom had never seen any reason to change it when she'd bought the place years before.

The three boys stopped on the sidewalk across the side street, squinting against the diesel smoke and dust as another big truck rumbled past. Wyatt grinned and patted his stomach, shouting over the truck's ground-shaking roar. "Yo! Smell that meat loaf! Best in Babylon!"

Dante sniffed the steamy aroma drifting out of the restaurant's open doorway. "I down!"

Wyatt gave a smirk. "Dishes, Buster-boy."

". . . Oh. Yeah."

"Aw," said Pook. "I help ya, man. What bruthas for."

"You just like a sista to him," snickered Wyatt.

The boys crossed the street and entered the café. The sounds of the sizzling grill, truck drivers' voices, and the constant clatter of plates and silverware blended in a comfortable clamor. Crockery rattled each time a truck pounded past. Lit by grimy windows and bare bulbs dangling from the wires, the room was just bright enough to invite you to chill, instead of glaring in your face like McDonald's decor and screaming at you to get your ass out the second you swallowed your last bite of food. There were booths along both windows, their leatherette benches a patchwork of silver duct tape, and a counter with round swivel stools lined the far wall. The middle of the room was a clutter of mismatched tables and chairs, while a digital jukebox blinked from one corner like a starship computer display. "Rat in the Kitchen," by UB-40, bumped through the meat-scented air. Fact was, there *were* rats in the kitchen, but they were as well fed and friendly as most of the customers. Even the winehead and the skeletal junkie nursing coffee and pie at the counter seemed contented.

Dante had heard of a restaurant called Big Mama's, but this one really should have been. Wyatt's mom might have been the biggest thing on legs in Oaktown . . . except for the cranes across the street.

Dante scoped the customers, wondering who'd played the reggae song. He felt his heart skip for a second, but in a good kind of way, hoping his dad had come back, but there were no other dreds in the room. Pook touched his shoulder.

"I know what you thinkin'."

Dante shrugged. "Well, he wasn't s'posed to be back till tomorrow."

Wyatt's mom squeezed herself through the kitchen doorway, a platter of meat loaf specials balanced on one hand. She had a voice to go with her size.

"Wyatt! Boy, where you been? Sassin' your teacher, gettin' detentions?"

Wyatt ignored the grins from some of the customers. "No, Mom!"

"Well y'all get yourself back there to busy this minute! Cheo been workin' his butt off ever since he got home!"

A crash came for the kitchen, followed by little-kid curses.

"Lord!" Wyatt's mom stopped for a second to spread the plates out at a table of truck drivers. "Wyatt! I swear that boy bust one more dish today, it comin' out *your* allowance! Now, git!"

"Okay!"

Wyatt sidled past his mother, who still managed to whop his behind with the empty platter the minute he turned his back. The other boys followed, and Wyatt's mom paused to give them a smile.

"Pook. Swear you gettin' more handsome every day. An', Dante, how you doin', son?"

"Cool, y'know, Miz Brown."

"No more of them nasty attacks?"

Dante's eyes flicked to Pook's for a second. "Naw."

"We gonna help Wyatt with the dishes," added Pook.

Mrs. Brown beamed. "Y'all good boys."

There came another crash from the kitchen.

"Lord!"

"CHEO DONE IT!" bawled Wyatt, sticking his head back through the doorway. "Dante! Pook! Get your asses in here!"

To Dante, the café's kitchen was probably the friendliest and most familiar place in the world, besides his own home. He followed Pook to the back of the room where the dishes were washed. Wyatt was down on his knees spitting curses and picking up pieces of two broken plates. His eight-year-old brother stood at the big stainless steel sink on a plastic milk crate that sagged and creaked under his weight. Cheo reminded Dante of one of those overstuffed little winged children who flew around naked in church pictures, except he was way too fat to fly. He just wore baggy red shorts and black Nikes, and glistened with sweat and dishwater like a roly-poly sea lion pup. Even his long braids were dripping. A small soap-spattered blaster sat on a shelf over the sink and bumped out a ganxta-rap song. A Snapple pink lemonade bottle stood beside it, and Cheo grabbed it with a grunt, mashing his belly against the sink rim as he stretched out his arm. He killed the bottle and burped, then turned to Dante. "Yo! Help me down, man. I way past suppertime 'cause of my butt-brain brutha!"

Wyatt struggled to his feet and dropped the broken plate pieces into a garbage can. "You busted that one on purpose, ass-wipe!"

"Did not, blowhole! . . . MOM!"

Mrs. Brown's voice echoed from the other room. "WYATT!"

"OKAY!" Wyatt pulled the little gun out from under his stomach and laid it way back on a shelf, then plopped down in a chair at an old table stacked with clean dishes.

"Yo, Pook. Snag me some loaf an' potatoes."

"Hey!" yelled Cheo, getting down from the crate with Dante's help. "You gotta wash them dishes, butt-breath!"

Wyatt grinned. "Dante gonna do that."

"No fair, man! Nobody wash for me when I get home from school!"

Wyatt shrugged. "Like Dante always sayin', life ain't fair in Babylon . . . boy."

Dante slipped the pack from his shoulders and stripped off his shirt. Then he kicked the crate aside and stepped to the sink as Pook returned like a waiter, balancing a heaping plate of food in one hand, with a dish towel draped over his arm. He set the plate in front of Wyatt with a flourish. "An', what will *mon-sewer* be drinkin' with his meal?"

"Mix me up some chicken-bottle, *garçon*."

Cheo's mouth opened. "MO—"

Pook clapped a hand over Cheo's mouth. Cheo wiggled and squirmed to get free, slippery and hard to hold. Wyatt pointed. "Yo, Dante. Toss me that, huh?"

Dante sailed the Snapple bottle to Wyatt, who sniffed it and grinned at his little brother.

"New flavor, man? Chicken-bottle Snapple? Ain't no wonder you been bustin' plates out the asshole."

Cheo stopped struggling, and Pook took his hand away.

"So?" said Cheo. "I'ma tell Mom who ate all the pie last week, suck-face!"

"Aw," said Wyatt. "We cut a deal, kid. Sit your ass down. We both have some supper while our slaves do the work. Yo, ponyboy! 'Nuther plate here for my brotherman."

Pook bowed. "Oh, sure, master. It be in my blood to serve."

"An' some more chicken-bottle," said Cheo, sitting down at the table across from Wyatt.

"Then get over here an' dry dishes," added Dante.

Pook went to the cooler and expertly mixed a bottle of Thunderbird with two Snapples, set them before the other boys, then got another plate of meat loaf for Cheo.

"Will there be anything else for the white folks?"

"Yeah!" said Dante. "Get your ass *over* here, fool! These dishes pilin' up!"

"I'se a comin', boss."

Cheo giggled around a mouth full of meat loaf. "In your pants!"

"CHEO!" Mrs. Brown came in with a platter of dirty dishes. "Swear I gonna wash out that filthy mouth of yours with Lysol someday!" She set the platter down on the drain board and smiled at Pook, who had tied a towel around his waist and joined Dante at the sink. "You never hear Pook talkin' like that."

"Yeah, Cheo," added Wyatt. "Pooky can be your role model. We dress you up in white silk pajamas an' sell you down at the bus station for ten bucks a trick."

"WYATT!" Mrs. Brown gave him a glare. "You ain't out-grown a good healthy mouth-washin' neither! Swear there been times when I trade the both of you in for a well-mannered boy like Pook."

Wyatt grinned at his little brother. "She always did want a girl."

Mrs. Brown scowled. "Ain't that the truth! Girls got *sense!*" She went back to the stove to prepare another platter.

Dante leaned over the sink to change stations on the boom box. "Ain't nuthin' on the air no more 'cept stupid-ass ganxta rap! I'ma bring one my reggae tapes tomorrow."

"*After* you get out rehab," reminded Wyatt.

"Aw, hell! I keep forgettin' 'bout that."

Cheo looked up from his plate. "*Dante* in rehab? For what?"

"It a special one," said Pook. "Heart therapy."

"Oh."

Dante leaned over again and thumbed the blaster's volume down, then cocked his head toward the kitchen doorway. "Listen, Pook. Somebody playin' 'Kingston Town.'"

"Yeah. Your dad like that one. Figure he back?"

Dante threw down the dishrag. "I'ma go check it out."

Wiping spatters of soap from his body, Dante walked through the kitchen and stood in the doorway, scanning the restaurant's front room. It was easy to spot the container-truck drivers; black, brown, Asian, or white, they always sat talking together. Dante sometimes wondered if they hung with each other when they weren't on the job. It was an interesting idea. There were some Vietnamese who were probably fishermen, and a wrinkled old Chinese guy who had been eating at the café a long time before Wyatt's mom bought it. He always ordered just tea and soup-of-the-day, and sometimes stared around as if caught in a time warp and wondering what had happened. The winehead and junkie were still at the counter . . . Wyatt's mom let them stay as long as they didn't nod off or puke . . . and a family of white folks who might have been tourists had taken a booth by the west-facing window. Dante studied them a moment: mommy and daddy and a pudgy-looking boy about his own age in black Machine jeans, hoodie sweatshirt, and spotless Adidas. Why white kids dressed hip-hop was a mystery. The boy's blue eyes caught sight of Dante and he flashed a peace sign, probably because of Dante's dreds. Dante signed back because Rasta were supposed to try and love everybody. He'd worn dreds since baby-hood, and his father had told him a long time ago that dredlocks often brought out the best or the worst in people who saw them.

It was now early evening, and the sun slanting in through the window made it hard to see the booths up front. Dante squinted, then felt his heart skip again when he saw a man's profile silhouetted in the sunlight.

"Dad!"

Dodging between the close-packed tables, Dante dashed across the room. The man saw him coming and spread his arms with a smile. Dante all but leaped into his father's lap . . . probably would have if there had been room in the booth. Boy and man locked arms around each other in a hug. Dante held tight to his dad, pressing his cheek to the man's and not caring about their dreds tangling or the white boy's openmouthed stare. The boy's parents looked startled for a second, but then dropped their eyes back to the menus.

"Dad! I *knew* you was back! 'Rat in the Kitchen' was playin' when I come in!"

The white boy's parents looked uneasy; both casting glances

toward the kitchen, where Mrs. Brown was just emerging with another big platter of specials.

The man moved aside to give Dante room. He was tall and lean, and, like Dante, it seemed as if his muscles had been added after his ebony skin had been fit. He had an angular face, further darkened by years in the sun, and his locks shaded from sepia to rich chocolate-brown, bushy and longer than his son's. A floppy blue denim cap kept them out of his eyes. He was dressed in faded old 501's and an equally well-worn chambray work shirt, streaked and stained with oil and gear grease. The shirt hung half-open, revealing the twin to Dante's beaded necklace. He gripped Dante's shoulders and studied him.

"Slow down, son. *Breathe*, boy. How you doin'?"

"Cool, y'know." Dante sucked deep breaths. As always, his dad smelled like man-sweat and diesel oil, and his hair was scented like the heavy old rope that tied ships to wharves. Kneeling on the bench, Dante glanced down at his own small-muscled body and wished he was strong like his father. But there was pride in the man's eyes as he looked at his son.

"Why you all soakin' wet?"

"'Cause he been washin' the dishes for my lazy boy," said Mrs. Brown, waddling over. "Lord, Matthew, I'm sorry. I meant to tell Dante you was here, but I been rushed off my feet all day. My boys tryin' to help all they can, but Lord knows what I wouldn't give for a sensible girl!"

Matthew smiled. "Ever think about another try at marriage?"

Mrs. Brown chuckled. "Little late in my life to go through all that again. One man runnin' off was enough for me." She winked. "An' you a sailor. What I look like, a fool? Too bad I just can't drive through stork-in-a-box an' put in an order an' have it my way."

"So, where was you, Dad?" Dante demanded.

Matthew smiled again. "Seein' a man about a dog. Tugboats run mostly on coffee, y'know." His smile faded a little. "Look at you, son, shakin' all over. Maybe we best see the doctor 'bout them pills."

Dante frowned. "You talkin' the ones cost three dollars a pop? Hell! Need me no punk-ass pills, Dad!" Then he smiled. "A good ole beer chill my butt right now."

Matthew glanced at Mrs. Brown. "Wouldn't want you riskin' your license."

Mrs. Brown laughed. "Cops don't come in here, Matthew. They know they ain't welcome. Like to end up the main ingredient in somebody's burger supreme." She glanced over at the white lady in the next booth. "Spill your water, honey? Hang on, I get you another glass."

"S'pose you best bring my son a beer while you at it, then," said Matthew.

"Rollin' Rock," added Dante. "It all natural." He glanced at the window as the woman waddled away: reflected in the glass was the white boy's look of pure envy and the unguarded frowns of his parents. Dante looked back at his father. "Wyatt into chicken-bottle. I can't stand the stuff."

"Mmm." Matthew considered his son. "'Member what the doctor say? 'Bout smokin' an' drinkin'?"

Dante heaved a huge sigh and counted on his fingers. "An' runnin', an' fightin', an' gettin' excited . . . an' just *livin'!* Hell, got to have me *some* choices, Dad!"

Matthew nodded slowly. "Mmm. Times I forget you be thirteen years old, now."

"Well, least that wack ole doctor didn't tell me not to go gettin' erections!"

Matthew chuckled. "'Spect that depend on what you gonna do with 'em."

"What Jah made 'em for," said Dante. Behind him, he heard the white people get up and leave. Mrs. Brown returned with a bottle of beer. Dante tilted it up and took a big gulp, then smacked his lips and puffed his chest. "Feel my heart now."

"Mmm. Well, you don't wanna go an' slow it down too much."

"Yo, Dad, that what I sayin' . . . 'bout them stupid pills. Got to take one to slow the sucka down, an' then another one to give it a kick in the ass again! Just like bein' on drugs! Don't wanna live like that!" Dante took another swallow, then set down the bottle and rolled it slowly between his palms. "Um . . . so, you gonna be home for a while now?"

Matthew sighed and took a sip of his coffee. "That why I come to see you today, son. We picked up another tow for Stockton. Gotta be leavin' tonight."

"Aw . . . hell!"

Matthew laid a hand on Dante's shoulder. "Listen, son. I be home for sure by Sunday. I can get the truck again. We can go to Marine World with Wyatt an' Pook like we was talkin'."

Dante sighed, staring at the bottle. "Yeah. That be cool. But . . . I just wish you could stay now, is all."

"I wish I could too, Dante."

Dante pushed the bottle away. "Dad? It always gonna be like this, you always workin' an' no time to do nuthin' else?"

Matthew was silent a moment. Like Dante, he rolled the coffee cup in his palms. Finally, he sighed. "Son, you know we don't got a choice. Gotta take any tows we can get. Bills don't stop just 'cause a man wanna spend some time with his son."

Dante shrugged. "Yeah. Only thing matter in Babylon be money!" He turned to face his father. "So, how long you got?"

"Plenty of time for supper with you."

Dante drew back the bottle and took a small sip. "That be cool. Um, I'ma go tell Wyatt an' Pook; 'cause of the dishes."

Matthew smiled once more. "Pook still stayin' with us?"

"Yeah. His parents don't want him around no more. They all cracked-out, an' he won't do . . . stuff . . . to score 'em money."

Matthew sighed again. "Babylon sell its own children, an' the price keep gettin' lower all the time." He glanced out the window toward the docks. "There money we always gettin' offered . . . for goin' outside to meet with some ship an' bring in more drugs to kill off our kids." He was quiet once more, then turned back to Dante. "Just one of them runs would pay for your operation."

Dante met his father's eyes, but then shook his head. "Rasta don't work for no CIA."

Matthew smiled. "Bob Marley say that."

"Yeah. But sometimes I wonder if just livin' in Babylon ain't workin' for 'em too." Dante slid from the booth, then paused. "Dad? I'ma come down to the boat after supper, help you cast off."

"Well, I got the truck outside, but it a long walk back, son. An' that place a war zone after dark."

"Everywhere is war, Dad. Bob Marley say that too. I be cool."

Pook was now shirtless at the sink and up to his elbows in dishwater. Wyatt was still forking meat loaf while Cheo sprawled back in his chair, legs spread wide and dangling, both hands on his belly, eyes shut, and a look on his face of pure pleasure. Dante slipped into his own shirt.

"Yo. I'ma eat supper with my dad."

"Oh, sure," said Pook. "It cool. I do the dishes."

"Well, after, I'ma go down the boat. Dad be leavin' again tonight . . . but he comin' back Sunday. Maybe we can all go to Marine World."

Wyatt nodded. "Okay. I let you slide, man. Today. I have supper an' then help pony-boy dry."

Pook frowned. "Yo, Dante. You gonna walk back from them docks all alone?"

Dante shrugged. "So?"

"So, I down with you, man."

Wyatt looked up. "So, who gonna wash?"

Pook smiled. "So, guess you is, Buster Brown."

Wyatt heaved a sigh. "Okay, but . . ." He glanced at Dante.

"This mean you still owe me dishes tomorrow, man."

Dante grinned. "I gots rehab tomorrow . . . fool."

"Aw, hell! Friday then, for sure!" Wyatt turned to Pook. "Yo, best pack my steel. Don't want y'all gettin' your asses capped so I gotta do dishes." He glanced at his little brother. "Too bad you couldn't been a girl like Mom always wanted."

Cheo scowled. "Too bad *you* couldn't been a cool homo-boy like Pook, 'stead of a stupid blowhole!"

4

The tugboat was ancient: sixty-five feet of rusty riveted iron patched in places with bolted-on plates. The eighty-foot wooden barge tied to the wharf astern of the tug looked even older. It was built out of planks that had weathered rat-gray and were bearded at the waterline with river grass and barnacles. Its name, *Amistad #3*, was painted in black on its battered sides. Chained on deck were seven old army-surplus bulldozers destined for farms somewhere up the Delta. The tug's name was *Bantu* in blood-red letters on bows and stern. It looked like it had been battling all of its life.

The short wharf was rotten and falling apart. Moss covered its creaking pilings and weeds grew tall on its mushy planks. Dante felt the whole structure sway underfoot as the barge nudged against it with a whimper of truck tire fenders. He watched with Pook as *Bantu's* two deckhands worked at the stern, securing the shackle pin of the barge's bridle to the tug's towline. Dante's father stood by the huge towing winch behind the engine room doghouse, ready to let out slack when *Bantu* cast off.

Dante shivered in the chilly Bay breeze and turned up the collar of his ragged Levi's jacket. Pook zipped his own old horse-blanket coat a little tighter. The night was clear, but moonless and dark. In the distance shone sodium floodlights at a refinery wharf that lit up a pair of oil-tanker ships, but the only light here was the yellowish glow of *Bantu*'s deck lamps and their dull reflection in the lapping black water below.

On *Bantu*'s stern, the deckhands finished with the shackle, then let the bridle slip overboard. Matthew looked up at the boys on the wharf as the deckhands took their places at the tug's bow and stern. "Ready?"

Dante raised a thumb. "Go for it, Dad!"

Crouching, he unwound *Bantu*'s stern line from a massive iron cleat as Pook ran down the wharf to untie the bow. Both boys dropped the heavy lines, which were snaked aboard by the deckhands, then dashed back up the wharf to cast off the barge.

Bantu's engine throttled up. Black smoke billowed from her stack to smudge the starry sky. Water thrashed creamy white beneath the tug's stern as the big propeller bit. Slowly, *Bantu* moved away from the wharf. Matthew let off the winch brake, and the drum revolved with a squeal, spooling out cable.

"Hurry, Pook!" panted Dante. He reached the barge's bow-line and whipped the heavy rope loose from its cleat as Pook ran on to untie the stern. *Bantu* was fifty feet from the wharf now, still unreeling cable. Dante leaped to *Amistad*'s deck and dropped the rope aboard.

"Bust it, Pook!" he shouted. "Dad gonna set at two hundred feet!" He turned toward the tug . . . about a hundred feet off now, coming up on one-fifty . . . *"Pook!"*

"I got it, Dante! Jump!"

The barge had already started drifting away, pushed by the current. Dante leaped the widening gap to the grassy wharf planks. *Bantu* was nearing two hundred feet out. Dante turned, seeing Pook still on *Amistad*'s stern.

"POOK! C'MON!"

There was a soft hiss as the tug's towline went taut and lifted partway out of the water. Droplets glittered like molten gold in the glare of the distant refinery lights. With an eerie silence for something so huge, the barge began to move, easing away from the wharf to follow the tug. Its sidelight slipped past like a big emerald eye.

"POOK!"

A shadow landed on cat feet beside Dante. "I was coilin' the rope, man! Ain't that what you s'posed to do on a boat?"

"Line," said Dante. "You coil the *lines.*"

"Oh. Sure."

Dante blew out a sigh, watching as *Amistad* moved off across the dark water and its white stern light came into view. "'Nuther damn minute an' you wouldn't got your ass off that thing till they tie up in Stockton tomorrow, fool!"

Pook grinned. "I thought it was just gonna be a three-hour tour."

Smiling, Dante looked out across the water as the barge swung slowly to trail the tug. Then he frowned and pointed. "Yo! Check that. Some stupid sucka gonna cut between *Bantu* an' her tow! You *never* do that!"

Pook watched with Dante, who stood scowling with his hands on hips as the ruby sidelight of a small boat crossed in front of the barge. The boat, big outboard snarling, was moving fast, kicking up silvery showers of spray as its bow slammed the Bay chop.

"Sucka sure in some kinda hurry," said Pook.

Dante scowled. "Maybe to his own funeral! That towline come up, it bust that little boat right in half!"

Four furious blasts sounded from *Bantu's* whistle. Dante nodded. "Skipper slowin' down, lettin' the towline slack so that stupid sucka don't hit it." Dante watched until the small boat's sidelight finally reappeared on the other side of the barge. "Look like the fool got away clean. This time. C'mon, Pook. Let's go home."

"Don't you wanna watch some more? We can see *Bantu* till it go round them ships over there."

"She, Pook, boats is always 'she.' An', don't wave. It be bad

luck. Wave a ship out of sight an' you might never see her again."
Dante started up the wharf with Pook at his side, passing a bar-
rier of boards and rusty oil barrels, then walking up a short pas-
sageway between two old warehouses and emerging onto a dim-
lit street lined with silent scrap yards and crumbling brick industrial buildings. Dante gave the street a careful check. "Best keep
the gun ready, Pook."

"Oh, sure."

The night breeze grew stronger, ruffling Dante's dreds as the
two boys headed up the buckled sidewalk.

"Stay out here by the gutter, Pook. Watch the shadows."

Pook nodded. "An' scope for Five-o, too. Sometimes they
park in a alley to sleep down here."

"Yeah. Don't feel up for gettin' curbed by them suckas neither.
They shove my dad around one time when he down here late
workin' on the boat. Didn't wanna believe that a black man could
be a engineer!"

"Dante?"

"Yeah?"

"You think you like workin' on a boat when you older?"

Dante slowed for a moment to check the black gap between
two buildings. "It hard work. You gots to fix my heart first."

"Oh, sure."

Dante eyed the shadows between two container trailers. "Dad
talk sometimes about cruisin' *Bantu* down to the Caribbean, where
Jamaica an' Haiti an' all them other pretty islands is. He say there
a lotta work down there for a tug, an' everythin' ain't buried in
Babylonian bullshit."

"Figure it make it that far?"

"*She,* man. Boats is always 'she,' 'member?"

"Funny. A tugboat look more like a homeboy. Know what I
sayin'? Like a rugged child, sorta."

Dante smiled. "Yeah. You right. An', 'course she'd make it.

With my dad runnin' the engine." Dante spit on the concrete. "'Cept it cost major money to get there . . . *Bantu* suck a lotta fuel." He frowned. "An' fifteen-hundred-dollar ambulance rides don't get us no closer to gettin' our butts out this crazy-ass place."

Dante sighed, jamming his hands into his jeans pockets. "Sometimes I think about all the stuff my dad could be doin' if I wasn't around to mess it all up."

Pook smiled. "He love you . . . fool."

Dante kicked a toe at the sidewalk. ". . . Yeah, but it just too bad he couldn't have a normal kinda son."

Pook grinned. "Mean, like me?"

"Oh, shut . . ." Dante stopped and stared up the street. "Car comin'! Fast!"

Pook shaded his eyes against a street lamp's glow. "Two of 'em! One a Five-o!"

Dante looked around as the cars roared down the street. The cop cruiser following the first now lit its strobes and bounced red and blue beams off the buildings. "Best hide! Here, Pook! Under this trailer!"

The boys dove beneath a container trailer, scuttling into the shadow between the two sets of tires and flattening themselves to trash-covered pavement under the axles. Pook squinted into the headlight glare of the fast-nearing cars.

"Wonder how come them pigs ain't usin' their siren?"

"Guy in the first car already know they after him."

Dante felt the concrete vibrate beneath him to the oncoming car's deep-throated thunder. The engine roar sounded somehow familiar. Both cars were doing about fifty as they blasted down a block of stacked containers. The cop cruiser seemed to be easily gaining. Then, Dante heard the first car shift gears. Its big engine bellowed an arrogant challenge. Rubber squealed, and the car seemed to drop on its haunches and wiggle its tail like a dare before shooting ahead as if it had a hyperdrive shunt under its hood.

Dante gave Pook a nudge in the ribs. "Whoa! Check that out, man! It like he just been playin' with them pigs!"

Pook raised up on his elbows. "Look! He throw somethin' out!"

"It a gun! That why he warp, so the pigs wouldn't see him throw it away!"

The first car was only a half block up from the hidden boys now. There was another squeal of tires as it cut close to the line of trailers. Something else was flung out—a black shape like a briefcase that skipped like a stone before sliding into the gutter.

"Hell!" hissed Dante. "It that punk-ass, Air Touch!"

"Too bad he gonna get away."

But then came another long screech of rubber as the Viper locked up its seventeen-inch tires and skidded under expert control toward the curb. Dante twisted around to see the car slide to a stop right in front of the trailer.

"Down, Pook!"

Seconds later, the cruiser came skidding sideways to a halt, blocking the Viper's escape. Both boys blinked as bitter tire smoke drifted on the breeze and burned their eyes. The cruiser's front doors burst open wide, the cops, both white, crouched behind them with pistols aimed through the open windows.

Air Touch seemed to know the right moves . . . which were no moves at all. He sat in the Viper totally still, both hands in plain sight on top of the wheel.

The cops exchanged glances, then the one who'd been driving reached in and shut off the flashing strobe lights.

"You!" he called to Air Touch. "Remove the keys from the ignition! *Slowly!* Toss them out on the street! Then open the door with the *outside* handle! Keep your hands where I can see them at all times! Step out of the car, then put both hands on top of your head!"

Air Touch did what he'd been told, still managing to look cool. He was wearing an expensive knee-length leather coat that looked as soft as black butter. His beepers showed bright at his waist as the coat spread open when he raised his arms and clasped his fingers together on top of his head.

"Bet they call for backup now," whispered Pook.

"'Course," Dante whispered back. "There only two white men with guns against one black boy. Prob'ly be a SWAT team here in a minute!"

But, both cops only stood up, still half-sheltered behind the car doors. "You!" called the first one again. "Turn around and face the sidewalk! *Slowly!* Place your hands behind your head! Get down on your knees! *Slowly,* nigger!"

Dante frowned. "Funny they ain't called for backup yet. An' they turn off their lights."

Pook looked thoughtful. "Mmm. Yeah. But, whatever happen, we gotta bail fast when they done with Air Touch. He gonna be back for his gun an' the package."

Dante glanced over his shoulder. "So, what you figure in that package, Pook?"

"Got to be rock. That the only thing he ever sell."

Air Touch was kneeling in the street now. Dante couldn't see his face, but could almost feel his satisfied smirk. The first cop covered the second as the man came cautiously up behind Air Touch, holstered his pistol, and cuffed Air Touch's hands behind his back. Both cops scanned the deserted street, then the second one went through Air Touch's pockets and came up with nothing but the big switchblade. He glanced at his partner, who shrugged, and then slipped the knife back into Air Touch's coat pocket and patted Air Touch's head in an almost friendly-looking way. The first cop now also holstered his gun and walked up in front of the kneeling boy.

"Okay, Sambo. Where's the money?"

Dante thought he saw Air Touch stiffen slightly, and there seemed to be an uneasy edge in his voice. "What you talkin' 'bout, money?"

The first cop frowned. "Strike one, boy." He nodded to the second, who picked up Air Touch's keys, went to the Viper, and gave the whole car a quick expert search, but shook his head. The first cop slipped the big club from his belt and smacked it on his open palm.

"Know that sound, *Rodney?* Here's a hint. Police across the country say, *use it!*"

Dante saw Air Touch go tense. The cop saw it too, and smiled. "No time for games, monkey. We know you were down here for a buy. Moving up in the world, aren't you? Where's the money?"

The club smacked the cop's palm once more, and Dante saw Air Touch's body jerk slightly in what Wyatt would call the "Fight or flight reflex." Now there was fear in his voice: "Six bills in my wallet, man. Take it."

The first cop sighed. "Strike two." He stepped around front of Air Touch. The second cop came up behind and also pulled his club. Air Touch's head was lowered: he stared down at the dirty pavement. With smirking gentleness, the first cop slipped the tip of his club under Air Touch's chin and raised his face.

"Look at me, ape. This ain't *Cops.* See any cameras around? Real easy to be a victim in a place like this."

Dante could smell Air Touch's fear, bitter on the breeze like the scorched-tire smoke. Air Touch could have killed him earlier that day, and yet Dante almost felt sorry for him now.

The second cop imitated the first, smacking his club on his palm while the first watched Air Touch's face, smiling when he winced. Still gentle, he put the club's tip against Air Touch's lips.

"Better do some thinkin', Sambo. It's not hard to figure out. Even for somebody with a monkey brain." Then the cop pulled back his club and wiped the tip on Air Touch's cheek.

"Minute's up, jigaboo. Now, where's the money?"

"Air Touch got balls, whatever else he is," whispered Pook when the boy didn't answer.

Dante shrugged slightly. "Got to figure it prob'ly ain't *his* money, man. Them pigs ain't gonna kill him, whatever else they do, but whoever the money belong to prob'ly would."

Pook shot a glance over his shoulder. "Oh, shit, Dante! You figure that package all fulla *money?*"

Dante felt sweat break out on his body. His throat went suddenly tight, his heartbeat faltered for a second, and it took effort to keep his voice steady even in a whisper. "Oh, man, Pook! What if it *is?*"

Pook's hand closed over Dante's. "Chill, brutha. Ain't nuthin' we can do now, 'cept wait."

Dante swallowed, dry as cotton, watching both cops raise their clubs. His own body jerked as the clubs whipped down and Air Touch screamed. Dante squeezed his eyes shut and jammed his hands over his ears. His own breath seemed beaten from his body, and his heart pounded loud in his chest. Hours seemed to pass, but it couldn't have been more than minutes when he finally opened his eyes again to see the first cop give Air Touch's curled-up body a final kick. The second cop knelt and took off the cuffs. Both men were breathing hard. Sweat shone on their pink-tinted faces in the cruiser's headlight beams. Air Touch lay totally still. Dante held his breath, ignoring the pain in his chest, as the second cop cautiously nudged the boy's form with the toe of his boot. Air Touch moaned softly.

The men exchanged glances again. Dante thought they looked slightly suspicious and uncertain of each other, like two little boys who had done a naughty thing together. Then the first cop forced a laugh. "Get his wallet. Six hundred's better than nothing."

The second cop looked slightly relieved. He got the money, then tossed Air Touch's wallet into the gutter. The first pulled a small book from his gun belt and a pen from his pocket.

"What'er you doing?" asked the second.

"Giving the jungle bunny a parking ticket." Grinning, the cop scribbled with the pen, then ripped off the ticket and stuck it under the Viper's windshield wiper blade. He laughed again. "Satisfy my white rage."

Pook's hand pressed Dante's once more. "Can you run?"

"I . . . think so."

"Then, soon's they gone, bail it, man. I get the package. An', be damn sure Air Touch don't see you!"

Dante concentrated on getting back his breath as the cops returned to their car and it squeaked off down the street. Pook was on his feet in a second, dashing away up the sidewalk, darting beneath the other trailer, then scrambling back out with the package. He waited, poised like a panther as Dante scuttled out onto the sidewalk and ran, then loped along easily at Dante's side. Then, Dante saw something shiny on the sidewalk ahead. Stumbling, he scooped it up as he ran past: Air Touch's gun! Pook noticed but said nothing, only running beside him with the package clutched under one arm.

Dante forced himself on for three more blocks before finally slowing to an exhausted walk. Under his jacket his T-shirt was sodden with sweat. He leaned on Pook the rest of the way home, catching his feet in cracks and staggering like a drunk little kid. Wyatt's mother's café was now closed for the night. The boys passed it and entered the weedy front yard of the second house. Pook helped Dante climb the steps to the porch. Dante stopped for a minute, bent over and clutching his knees to get air, then dug keys from his pocket and gave them to Pook. He had slipped Air Touch's gun down the front of his jeans, and, warm from his skin, it felt somehow reassuring. Pook seemed tense, not taking time to check out the package there on the porch. He unlocked the barred security screen and the plywood-sheathed door and gently pushed Dante inside, then scanned the street before slipping in after and locking the locks. Finally, he eased back the curtain on the door's small window and stood looking out while Dante caught his breath. A car cruised past, dope-rhymes bumping deep, but it was only a rusty old low-rider Buick.

Dante ripped open his jacket and mopped his face with the tail of his shirt. "We done it, Pook! Air Touch was just layin' there with his face in the gutter! No way he coulda seen us!" Dante stepped to the window and gazed back toward the distant docks. "He prob'ly *still* layin' there, way them pigs done him!" Dante shook his head and turned to Pook. "I know it stupid, but I almost feel sorry for him."

Pook's face looked thoughtful in the dim glow filtering through the small square of glass. After a moment he shrugged. "He playin' *their* game, man. An' he lose this round. Wanna take his gun back? Or . . ." He patted the package. "This?"

Dante shook his head and sucked a deep breath. "'Course not! Let's get upstairs an' check out the money!"

Pook seemed to consider, glancing down the dark first-floor hallway. "What about Wyatt?"

"What you mean?"

"Well, he our homey. Seem like we oughta clue him."

Dante brushed drops of sweat from his dreds. ". . . Well . . . he hate climbin' stairs . . . an', maybe he doin' his homework?"

Pook cocked his head. "Yo. What you sayin', Dante?"

Dante sighed. "Nuthin'. You right man, he our homey. Let's go tell him."

The house had been converted years before into three separate apartments. Wyatt's family lived on the ground floor, and Dante and his dad on the third. The landlady had the second-floor rooms.

Dante and Pook went down the hall past the steep spiral staircase and stopped at a door. The sounds of an old *Family Matters* rerun seeped through the heavy oak panel. Dante gave Pook a glance, then knocked. A second later Mrs. Brown's bellow demanded to know who it was.

"Me, Miz Brown," called Dante.

"WYATT! GET THE DOOR, HONEY!"

Slightly fainter, probably from his room, came Wyatt's roar. "CHEO!"

"NO WAY, BLOWHOLE! I GOT NO CLOTHES ON! MOM!"

"WYATT!"

"WHO IS IT?"

"DANTE, HONEY!"

"OKAY!"

Heavy barefooted steps crossed the carpet inside, and three locks clacked back on the door. Wyatt pulled open the panel and peered into the lightless hallway. "S'up, kids?"

Wyatt's belly hung down so far in front that only from a side or back view could his ragged boxers be seen. He gave Dante a scoping. "What happen, man? You get another attack or somethin'?"

"Naw." Dante jerked his chin upward. "C'mon, Wyatt. Pook an' me got somethin' to show you."

"Aw, I ain't up for them stairs tonight. Just c'mon in my crib."

Pook leaned over Dante's shoulder. "No. This be deep, Wyatt. Y'all c'mon up with us."

Wyatt studied his friends a moment more, then sighed. "Okay." He glanced back into the room. "Mom, I goin' up to Dante's."

"Your homework all done?"

"'Course." Wyatt stepped into the hall and pulled the door shut behind him. "Okay. Whattup?"

"My crib, man," said Dante, turning to follow Pook.

Muttering, one hand on the back of his boxers to keep them from slipping off, Wyatt struggled up the staircase behind the other boys. Reaching the third floor, Pook unlocked the door to Dante's apartment, then stepped aside for Wyatt and Dante to enter. Dante snapped the wall switch and an ancient brass floor lamp with a tasseled gold shade came on in one corner, casting a warm yellow glow. Like the others below, the apartment had a pair of small bed-rooms and a tiny kitchen, all reached by a hall from the living room. The ceilings were high in Victorian style, and ornate wood-en lintels adorned every doorway like dark gingerbread. Lath peeked in places where plaster had fallen from ceilings or walls. A colorful Turkish carpet covered most of the living-room floor. There was a tattered sofa draped in an olive-drab army blanket, and an old brown leather chair, its arms carved like lion paws. Instead of a footstool there was a huge iron piston from a Superior diesel. Other bits of marine machinery were scattered about: intri-cate objects of copper and brass that were just cool to look at or touch even if you didn't have a clue what they were. Board-and-brick bookshelves lined one wall, holding rows of flea-market paperbacks and dog-eared technical manuals. Magazines covered the coffee table, their titles ranging from *Workboat* and *Ships* to *Ebony Man* and *The Source*. The sofa and chair faced a Philco TV that sat on a low chest of drawers. The apartment had a sort of far-away smell: a mixture of leather and rope and diesel and tar that somehow conjured a *déjà vu* feeling of distant seaports. Fainter, were the man- and boy-scents of jeans and sweat and dredlocks.

The air was chilly, and Dante shivered in his sweat-soaked clothes. He went over to light a cast-iron gas fire that crouched in a corner on little clawed feet. Wyatt didn't seem to notice the cold, only padding to the couch and plopping down.

"So? Like I say, whattup?"

Pook said nothing, only locked the door. Dante glanced at him, and then at the package under his arm. Wyatt noticed the package now, and cocked an eyebrow. For a few seconds the only sound in the room was the gentle hiss of the gas flames. Finally, Dante slipped off his jacket and shirt and hung them on a hook above the fire, then came to the couch. He pulled the big pistol from his jeans and laid it on the coffee table before sitting down beside Wyatt.

The fat boy's eyes went wide. "The hell!" He picked up the gun and examined it carefully. "This a damn .357! Stainless-steel Smith & Wesson! How . . . ?"

Dante's look cut him off. Pook came over and dropped the package on the tabletop. Wyatt still held the gun, but his eyes went to the package and then to each of the other boys.

"Okay. This deep for sure! What you two been doin' tonight?"

But, Dante was only staring at the package. Seen for the first time up close and in the light, it seemed the wrong shape for what he'd expected. It was wrapped in what looked like a black plastic garbage bag, and crossed like a Bible with silver duct tape, but it wasn't the right size for bundles of bills.

And . . . he recalled the loud thump of it hitting the table . . . it was way too heavy!

Dante drew back and stared up at Pook. "That ain't money!"

Wyatt's mouth dropped open. *"Money?"*

Pook's eyes were unreadable, but his face looked sad. He shook his head slowly. "No, brutha. It ain't."

Dante felt a crinkly, little-kid-gonna-cry feeling in his nose. His own eyes narrowed to accuse. "You *knew* that! The minute you picked it up! So, why you bring it here?"

Pook blew air and shrugged out of his coat. His solid shoulders and arms gleamed like burnished bronze beneath the tight tank top. He crossed the carpet to hang his coat above the fire, then turned and shrugged. "I don't know, man. It like, once I pick it up, I couldn't put it down again."

Wyatt's eyes shifted between the other boys. "Okay, you two! Come correct! *Now!*"

The fire was warming the room. Pook peeled off his shirt and stood silently with his back to the flames like some chiseled sculpture guarding a gate, while Dante told Wyatt what had happened. The only sound when Dante finished was the gentle hissing of gas.

Wyatt put down the gun and gazed at the package for a few

minutes. The other boys' eyes followed his. Finally, he gave a slight shrug. "Got your blade, Dante?"

"Huh?"

Wyatt spread his hands. "Yo. We still don't know what in there."

Dante scowled. "Oh, get real, fool! Nuthin' but goddamn crack, all it is!" He swung eyes now hard to Pook. "So, what we gonna do, man, sell it at school?" He turned back to Wyatt and jerked a box knife from his jeans pocket. "Here! Go ahead an' open it! Then we dump the shit down the toilet!"

Wyatt took the knife, thumbed up the blade, then regarded the package thoughtfully. "Lotta money there if it concrete candy. Couple grand, maybe."

Again, Dante felt tears trying to start. He savagely wiped at his eyes. "Hell, man! Two grand ain't enough!"

He shut his mouth, feeling the other boys' eyes turn to him in something like the sympathy he didn't want.

"For your operation," Pook said softly.

Dante faced Pook in sudden defiance. "Yeah! For my goddamn operation! The one I prob'ly ain't gonna live long enough to get!" His chest heaved a moment, but then he shrugged and sank back into the sofa cushions. "Aw, go on! Open it, Wyatt! Then we flush it down the sewer where it belong!" He brushed clumsily at his eyes again. "Y'know, if it really been money, I'da shared it with both you."

Pook nodded. "We know that, man."

Dante leaned his head back and stared at the cracked plaster ceiling as Wyatt carefully made a slit down the side of the package, then peeled back the plastic.

"Hell!"

Dante sat up straight. "What?"

Pook had tensed, and now came almost warily across the room, eyes fixed on the package as if it was a ticking bomb. Dante leaned forward, his own eyes widening as Wyatt finished pulling away the black covering. Inside were smaller packages of thicker, clear plastic. All were packed as solid and bricklike as Pook's jutting pecs, with white powder that had a faint sparkle.

". . . Oh." Was all Dante could say. Then, "That what crack made of."

Wyatt nodded. "Yeah. An' you could make a whole goddamn truckload of crack outta what here! 'Less it go up some white basehead's nose first!"

Pook crouched by the table like a cat come upon something dead. "This wasn't for white people, man. Not with Air Touch in the mix. This for cookin' up rocks to make more little crackheads like Jinx."

Dante slipped from the sofa, sinking to his knees on the floor, elbows on the tabletop, chin in hands, gazing at the packaged powder. He felt his heart, still unsteady from the run, falter a little. He might have damaged it more, and for what? To bring *this* into his home! And yet he couldn't seem to take his eyes off the stuff.

"Must just come in," he murmured. "From some ship outside the Gate, an' then on a boat to the docks." He glanced at Pook. "Maybe that one we seen tonight cuttin' in front of the barge."

Wyatt nodded again. "Got to be what it is. Just like you say. That why Air Touch was down there. An' why them cops tryin' to jack him for money."

"Mmm," said Pook. "'Cept they come too late an' didn't know he already make the buy."

Dante still stared at the powder, somehow fascinated. He had to swallow to make his voice work. "Um, so what you figure them pigs woulda done if they found this on Air Touch? Or, even just layin' there in the street?"

Wyatt shrugged. "Pigs like them? What you think, man? They woulda just sold it somewheres. *They* gots connections, believe!"

Dante's right hand drifted to his chest, a fingertip feeling his heartbeat. "Figure they woulda sold it to other white people?"

Pook snorted, his nose wrinkling. "They woulda sold it to *anybody* got the bucks!"

Wyatt was looking thoughtful once more. "They be a lot more like to sell it down here. Less chance of somebody talkin'." He sighed and let his big rolly body slump back on the sofa before adding, "An' it only kill more of us."

As out on the street, hiding under the trailer and sensing Air Touch's fear, Dante felt his mouth go cottony dry. He swallowed again, his voice coming husky. "What you figure it worth?"

Pook tensed as if ready to spring, eyes flicking to Dante's and searching. "I'ma dump it down the toilet, man. Right now!"

He reached for the packages, but Dante caught his wrist across the tabletop. "No! Wait, man! *Think!*"

Pook might have easily shaken off Dante's fragile fingers, but he hesitated. "Think about what, Dante?"

"Choices, man! Choices we ain't got!" Dante threw Wyatt a pleading look. "How much you figure this worth, man? C'mon, Wyatt, give a clue! Enough for my operation, huh? Easy!"

Dante turned back to Pook, still holding his wrist but letting his grip go gentle. "An', what about med school, man? You know yourself that don't come cheap! I sayin', think about choices, bruthas!"

Pook's chest expanded in a deep breath that sighed out slowly and seemed to soften him. Dante let go, and Pook sank back to a crouch on the floor. He crossed his arms on his knees, letting his hands hang loose like paws. The fingers of one moved over his wrist where Dante had held it. "Maybe I was thinkin' 'bout that when I pick the shit up."

Wyatt stared at the two other boys for a second, then scowled. "Yo! The hell you two fools all about? You want this crap cooked an' a ton of it out on the street . . . *our* street?" He grabbed Dante's shoulder. "This shit make Jinx what he is, man! Think about that!"

But Dante shook his head, still watching Pook. "Jinx in rehab."

A short snicker escaped. "I even goin' with him tomorrow. To help him get clean."

For all his loose bulk, Wyatt moved fast, lunging to grab the edge of the table, flipping it over as Pook leaped out of the way, magazines and packages of powder scattering across the carpet. Lurching to his feet, Wyatt grabbed two of the packages. "C'mon, Pook!" he yelled. "Let's dump 'em! . . . *Pook!*"

Pook had scrambled up but now only stood, his arms hanging loose at his sides. He looked strangely helpless. His eyes shifted from Dante to Wyatt and then back again.

"Hell!" bawled Wyatt. He grabbed another package.

"NO!" Dante flung himself onto the floor, rolling, snatching the pistol, and then recovering in a crouch to aim it at Wyatt. "Don't touch 'em, man! Put 'em down! . . . Wyatt . . . goddamnit, man, *put 'em down!*"

The fat boy froze, a package in each hand and a look of amazement on his face. "Dante. Stop it, man. You . . . you scarin' me! This stuff *evil!*"

Tears glistened suddenly in Dante's eyes, like black ice for a second before they brimmed over and ran down his cheeks. He clutched the big silver gun in both hands, trying to hold it steady. His voice came husky again: "Please, Wyatt. Listen! *Choices*, man! Please!"

He glanced at Pook, who still hadn't moved, then turned back to Wyatt. "Listen! This *is* money, an' money mean choices! Wyatt, *listen!* What's money? Can you eat money? Can you wear it? Can it keep you warm when it cold out? Can it make you better when you sick? Hell, no! It only what money *buy* that keep you alive in Babylon!"

He pointed with the pistol. "Yo! You sayin' *this* stuff evil, man? What about money? You sayin' people don't kill an' die over money? You sayin' money don't make people hurt . . . like, money ain't the reason kids starvin' to death all over the world . . . an'

Jinx be a addict, an' Radgi livin' on the street . . . an' . . . I dyin' a little bit more every day?"

Carefully, Dante let go of the gun with one hand and picked up a package. "So, what if this *was* money, Wyatt? What if this was paper 'stead of powder? Would you take it? *'Course* you would, man! You take paper all covered with people's blood an' trade it for stuff *you* need to live! Hell, we got no choice!" He held out the package as if in offering. "*This* the only thing count in Babylon! It mean we can play in the game an' don't gotta be victims no more. An' you goddamn well know it!"

Dante turned to Pook. "Please, man. All I axin' is we think awhile! We . . . we can always flush it. Any ole time! We got that choice too!" Dante sniffled, feeling snot running down his lip, but afraid to let go of the gun and wipe it away. "Yo, Pook. What if we just sold it to white people? Y'know . . . them same sorta suckas who bringin' here anyway? All the best drugs uptown! Everybody know! We could do it, man! We could use Babylon's own game against 'em for once! I know we could!"

Dante turned once more to Wyatt. "Please, brutha. Let's think, okay? Just till tomorrow, okay? That all I axin'.."

Wyatt took a slow breath, and Dante wondered how a boy's small skeleton could support all the weight he seemed to be carrying. Wyatt let the packages drop to the floor.

"I'ma go home now." Wyatt turned his back on Dante, not seeing him lower the gun and finally put it down on the carpet. Pook faced Wyatt as the fat boy passed him.

"Um, Wyatt? That all we gonna do, man . . . just think awhile."

Wyatt nodded, his voice strangely quiet. "Sure, Pook. See you in the mornin'.."

Pook went over and pulled Wyatt's small gun from his coat pocket. "Here, man. Thanks for lettin' us pack it."

Wyatt took the little pistol without looking at it. "Sure." He walked to the door. The clicks seemed loud in the stillness as he unfastened the locks. Then he stopped, halfway out, and turned to face Dante, holding the gun, its muzzle aimed harmlessly skyward. "Babylon make it so I got to carry this. But I still got a choice who I use it on."

The door closed softly. there came the creaking and pops of the fat boy's heavy steps descending the staircase. Dante stayed on the floor, amid the mess of scattered magazines and packages of powder. Slowly, he lifted his eyes to Pook. "Lock the door."

Pook sighed. "Wipe your face, Dante. You lookin' like a snot-nose little kid." He went to the door and fastened the bolts.

Dante set the coffee table back on its feet, then carefully stacked the packages before starting to gather the magazines. Pook came over to help. When that was done, Dante remained on the floor, cross-legged, chin in hands, gazing again at the powder. Pook watched him a moment, then sat down at his side. Gently, he slipped an arm over Dante's shoulders.

"So, what we gonna think about, brutha?"

Dante felt comforted by Pook's closeness, but caught himself wondering if he would sit this way with Pook if there was anybody else to see. Except when they'd been little, he couldn't remember Pook ever touching him much when there was anyone else around, though he couldn't recall ever telling him not to.

"Everythin' happen so fast, Pook. I need me a beer."

"Axe me, you be needin' some sleep a lot more'n a beer."

Dante shrugged, feeling Pook's hard-muscled warmth against him. "How I sleep now? I needin' me somethin' to help. Don't you?"

"So, how 'bout some hot chocolate?"

Dante made a face. "Get real."

Pook studied Dante a moment more, then finally nodded. "Mmm. We could prob'ly axe Wyatt to boost us a couple brews."

Dante faced the other boy. "Um, you figure he pissed, Pook? I really didn't mean to go pointin' that gun at him. It just sorta . . . *happened.*"

"Oh, sure. I think he know that. We all been homeys too long for him not to." Pook smiled. "Today, when you hit me . . . that just sorta happen too, didn't it?"

"Yeah . . . maybe it got somethin' to do with hormones."

"Yo. I s'posed to be the doctor."

Dante reached out to touch a package with a fingertip. "We oughta get us somethin' slammin', like Eightball."

Pook's forehead creased and he took his arm away. "Y'all been through a lot today, Dante."

"Oh, hell, Pook, don't go startin' with that 'bad for my heart' bullshit. *Everythin'* in Babylon be bad for your heart." Dante got up. "Yo, we can go score from Kelly."

Pook glanced at a brass ship's clock on the wall above the bookshelves. "It almost nine, Dante, an' we still ain't done our history homework."

"Forget it, man. Miz Tyehimba think I a crackhead now anyways. She ain't gonna trip if I miss a 'signment for once."

"But how we gonna pay Kelly?"

"There be money in the kitchen Dad always leave."

"But that be for stuff you need, Dante."

"Well, I *need* me a forty-ounce, man."

Pook pulled a bill from his jeans. "Here. This my 'homo-boy' green. S'pose it oughta get used therapeutically."

Dante smiled a little. "Thanks, man." He started for his room to get a dry shirt, but stopped in the hallway entrance and stared back at the coffee table. "Yo! What we gonna do with that? We got to hide it somewheres!"

Pook got to his feet. "Why? Your dad ain't comin' back till Sunday."

". . . Yeah, but what if somebody bust in while we gone?"

"Hell, Dante, ain't nobody never bust in here before."

"Yeah . . . but what if somebody did? Yo. I stash it under my mattress!"

Pook smiled faintly. "Oh, sure, an' that the first place they look."

". . . Well . . . in the fridge, then . . . bchind the frozen food."

"That be the second place they look."

Dante's eyes scanned the apartment almost fearfully. "But, it got to be hid somewheres!"

"So, put it in your underwear drawer, man. Only a homo like me look in there."

The liquor store was a ramshackle wooden building, two stories tall, on a dim-lit street corner. It was practically paintless, and its old neon sign buzzed and flickered in fits. Only the bars on its window seemed in good shape. The cracked glass behind them was smothered with posters for second-batch beer and first-quality malt. As always there was a winehead passed out on the sidewalk in front and a handful of wannabe G's clustered around a street lamp pole. They were maxed and loud, and sucked from paper bags that held bottles of T-bird or malt. Three boys about fifteen or sixteen stood by the doorway in shouldertap poses. They gave Dante hard looks meant to scare off competition, but saw Pook's powerful frame and the warning in his eyes and stepped silently aside to let him and Dante pass.

The room was small and narrow and higher than it was wide. Two big bulbs burned brightly from the ceiling. Shelves and racks to one side were packed with bags of chips and pretzels and peanuts, along with candy bars and gum. There was a large selection of licorice too, and one shelf was devoted to condoms and toothpaste and disposable razors, while another displayed movies for rent with titles that ranged from *The Lion King* to *Love Games for Passionate People*. A counter ran along one wall, and there was a small glass-topped freezer of Eskimo Pies and Popsicles. Anything that contained a trace of alcohol — including cough syrup — was guarded by glass or wire mesh on shelves behind the counter. The beer and cold malt and chilled cheap wine lived in a big wheezing cooler.

The thin light-brown man at the register looked warily up from his paper as the boys came in and the door sensor bonged, but then smiled, showing gold.

"Ah. Dante, Pook. Wha'sa up?"

"Yo, Mister Pak," said Dante. "Kelly home?"

The man bowed slightly. "Kelly is upstairs. And, how is your father?"

"Cool y'know. They been gettin' a lotta tows."

"And, your operation? Closer to having?"

Dante glanced at Pook, then shrugged. "Still workin' on it."

Mr. Pak gave Pook a smile. "You getting to be handsome young man."

Pook grinned. "Ain't much of a point-spread on that." He pointed to the Korean newspaper open on the countertop. "Y'all find you a lady yet?"

Mr. Pak ran a finger down the columns of Korean print. "So many choices."

"Prob'ly a lot more'n I gots."

Mr. Pak shrugged. "You are young. Many choices in life, if you look for them." His almond eyes narrowed as he turned to point at the doorway and the rowdy crew gathered outside. "They do not think they have choices, but there is no wall around this city, or soldiers to keep them from leaving. They *choose* to come here every day. They choose to curse me, to steal, to beg. They cry 'victim,' but what do they know of the hunger and poverty in my land?" The man shrugged, then turned back to Dante with a smile. "You once told me a Rastafarian saying, 'In the abundance of water the fool is thirsty.'"

Dante considered that. "But, sometimes even water cost money. An', didn't you have help when you come here, Mister Pak? What I axin' is, wasn't there a sorta Korean community thing?"

"Ah. And why is there not a black community 'thing'? Your

people have had many years to learn traditional American values."

Dante sighed. "Yeah. I hear what you sayin'."

The boys bowed, then passed through a curtain of beads behind the beer cooler and climbed a set of squeaky box stairs to a peeling old door. Sirens and TV gunfire sounded from inside. Dante knocked, but there was no answer. A cop-voice yelled, "Three strikes you're out, loser!"

"Must be talkin' to us," Dante muttered. He knocked again. The TV muted, and there came the squeak of sofa springs and a padding of bare feet. Kelly dragged open the door, which scraped in a groove it had scooped in the floorboards. He wore just old boxers, his golden-toned body more like a barrel than actually fat, and his shaggy black hair hanging in front of his eyes.

"Yo, kids. S'up? C'mon in."

The tiny apartment was cluttered but clean, and the faint scent of *kimchi* lingered in the air. There was way too much furniture, old but surprisingly good, and seeming mostly unused except for the sofa that faced a Sanyo TV. Kelly led the other boys to the couch. The coffee table in front was a piled mix of American and Korean magazines, including what looked like some Asian hip-hop. Kelly's schoolbooks and binder were stacked among them, along with a half-empty bottle of Kirin.

"Bet he done *his* homework," said Pook, sitting down.

"Oh, shut up," said Dante, sitting beside him.

Pook touched a small puckered scar on Kelly's side. "So, how my work holdin' up, man?"

Kelly grinned. "Starts achin' just before a rain." He went to a fridge in the corner and returned with two more Kirins. "I just ate the last pizza roll. Sorry."

"S'cool," said Dante, taking the bottle and drinking deep. "We come to make a buy."

Pook sipped from his own bottle. "Ain't this a drink, man?"

Dante poked him. "I said, shut up."

"Oh, sure."

Kelly spread his hands. "I all outta Kry, man. Wyatt got the last of it today."

"Naw. We wanna score some malt."

Kelly raised an eyebrow. *You?*

"Yeah! There some kinda law against it?"

"Well, I just thought . . . 'cause of your heart. . . ."

"To hell with my heart, man! So, what you got?"

Kelly shrugged. "Anything y'all want. But, we got a special goin' on for Crazy Horse this week. Kickin' brew."

"All come from the same donkey anyways," said Pook.

"Let's do this," said Dante, giving Pook a frown.

"Sure," said Kelly. "How many y'all want?"

"Best make it three," said Dante.

Kelly picked up his own bottle and drained it. "Down. But, it cost ya two Lincolns."

"Yo!" said Pook. "Thought y'all just now say it on special!"

Kelly grinned. "Well, that *my* special, kid."

"Oh, hell," muttered Dante, killing the Kirin and pulling Pook's twenty from his pocket. "Here, damnit."

Kelly grinned again, then padded to where his overalls lay on a chair and returned with ten dollars' change. "So, y'all down with the program, kids. Cruise round back. Them doggies be waggin' their tails at the top of the steps by the time you get there."

"*Cold* ones," said Pook, draining his own bottle before getting up.

Kelly smiled. "'Course. Y'all know where I live."

Pook went back to the door, but Dante rose and moved close to Kelly, lowering his voice. "Um, you do any kinda guns 'sides them cheap Chinese things?"

Kelly cocked his head. "Sometimes. Y'all be surprised how many G's come round wantin' to deal a Colt for some Colt. So, whattup, Dante?"

"I might got one I wanna sell."

Kelly gripped Dante's shoulders a moment and scoped him up and down. "Yo, kid. You sure you the same Dante I see at school today? First you smokin', then you suckin' licorice in class, an' now you here buyin' malt an' dealin' steel."

Dante shrugged, frowning a little. "People change, man."

"Sometimes. But usually not this fast."

Dante's frown deepened, and he shot a quick glance over to where Pook waited. "Yo. I got me a .357. Stainless steel, S an' W. What it worth?"

Kelly considered. "Mmm. Majortime regulator. I could go three bills tonight. Maybe more if you wanna leave it on commission."

Pook had opened the door and now stood half out on the landing. "Yo, Dante. It gettin' near ten."

Dante leaned close to Kelly again. "I let you know, man. Tomorrow in history. Okay?"

"Sure. Might even have us a buyer by then."

Dante gave Kelly a quick brother-shake, then headed for the door.

"Carefully, kid," Kelly called after him.

Dante and Pook went down the stairs, said good night to Kelly's father, then left the store and walked around the corner to the alley in back.

"Maybe Too Short was right," said Dante as they headed into the alley's black mouth. "There really is money in the ghetto, if you know where to look."

Pook shook his head. "You mean, which brutha or sista you wanna burn! An', Too Short never made him no money in the ghetto, made it all spittin' rhymes 'bout the ghetto, an' then got his ass out!"

The boys passed by Dumpsters and garbage cans, then climbed the liquor store's backstairs. Outside the door at the second-floor landing was a big paper bag. Pook picked it up and checked the three bottles inside.

"They cold?" asked Dante.

"Better be! Like Kelly say, we know where he live!"

They started back down the staircase when a kid-voice called from the shadows underneath, a high-husky tone: "Dante?"

Dante stopped and peered over the railing. "Radgi?"

"Yeah."

Dante glanced at Pook, then leaned over again. "S'up, man? Why you under . . . oh. Guess that your crib, huh?"

"Sometimes. There's a lot of cardboard boxes. I can make a little house."

Dante wasn't sure if Radgi was joking or not. He reached the bottom step as the kid emerged from behind a Dumpster. Radgi's coat was buttoned tightly against the night cold, and Dante saw that the pockets were empty now.

"Um, you score enough cans to eat good today, man?"

"Yeah. I even went to Burger King tonight. But the money you brothers gave me helped. Thanks."

"Oh," said Dante, suddenly wishing there was something else he could say. "Um, see ya round, I guess."

Radgi lifted a hand in a small good-bye wave, and Dante saw him shiver as a breeze sighed in from the street. He remembered Radgi touching his hand after school: that feeling of warmth, and, strange as it seemed, a sense of caring. And there had been real concern in those big bronze-green eyes after what Air Touch had done. It was funny to think that Radgi, with more than enough problems of his own, could afford to let himself into anyone else's pain. Dante started to wave back, then hesitated. *Wave a ship out of sight and you might never see her again.*

"Um, Radgi? Wanna come home with us tonight? You could sleep on the couch, an' even take a bath."

Radgi seemed a little unsure, and Dante wondered if maybe the boy was uncomfortable because of Pook, like a lot of dudes were. But Radgi wasn't even looking at Pook. It was too dark to really see Radgi's eyes, but Dante could feel that green-tinted gaze searching his face.

"What about your parents, Dante?"

"I only gots my dad, an' he gone till Sunday."

Radgi's expression seemed to take on a faraway look. "We used to live in a house with a bathtub . . . a great big huge bathtub on feet."

Dante found himself slightly surprised that Radgi hadn't accepted his offer at the speed of light. "That what we got, man. Feet an' all."

"Yo," said Pook. "Did y'all have a boat, Radgi? To play with in the tub?"

Dante shot Pook a look, but Radgi only giggled. "Is that a doctor question?"

Pook smiled. "Naw. I just axin'."

Radgi looked suddenly shy. "I was little then. I think I had a duck."

Pook nudged Dante. "So did you, man."

Dante felt his face grow warm. "The hell! I had me a *boat*, man! A little tugboat my dad give me! The same one what still in my room, an' you know it!"

Pook only smiled again. "I 'member the duck, back in the day. You just don't, is all."

Dante turned back to Radgi, a little annoyed to be talking this sort of stuff with a homeless kid in an alley . . . a kid he was trying to care for! "Like I told you today, we always been homeys," he said, hoping that would explain something.

Radgi smiled. "That must be cool, growin' up all your life with somebody. So, was Wyatt always your homey too?"

Dante felt a momentary sadness. It had been a strange day: beating up one of his friends and turning a gun on the other. "Yeah, always." He made himself shrug. "So, you wanna come with us or not? It your choice, man."

Radgi nodded. "Yeah, Dante. An', thanks."

The ship's clock read 23:20. The TV was tuned to a channel that played ancient movies till dawn. The film showing now was called *The Flight of the Phoenix*: a big, old-time airplane had just crashed in the middle of a desert and it didn't look like anyone was coming to rescue the victims.

Dante, Pook, and Radgi all sat on the couch, Dante in the middle. One empty forty-ounce stood on the coffee table, and a second bottle, half-gone, was being shared. The gas fire hissed in the corner, filling the room with a comfortable warmth that seemed all the more friendly because of the flickering flames. Like Radgi and Pook, Dante had his bare feet on the table, the fire's heat flowing over his toes. Laid back with the bottle in hand and a buzz between him and the world, Dante could almost put Babylon out of his mind. He turned to Radgi, who hadn't said much since they'd gotten home. "So, what y'all thinkin' 'bout, man?"

Radgi's gaze seemed fixed on the TV screen, where the broken airplane lay in the sand. Dante and Pook had stripped off their shirts along with their shoes, but Radgi had just shed his jacket. Dante noticed that beneath the grimy tee, Radgi's tummy looked awkward and out of proportion. Despite the chubbiness of his chest, he just didn't have the backup bulk of a normal fat kid. His cocoa-brown arms were smooth and almost childlike in their lack of muscle. Dante had also noted that he kept his jacket within easy reach on the floor, just as he kept the greasy X cap clamped to his woolly-wild bush of rust-colored hair. Dante wondered if always being ready to leave was a sort of survival skill homeless kids learned.

Radgi's eyes stayed on the TV. "I wonder where that is?"

Dante hadn't been paying much attention to the movie. He studied the scene now. "Look like Egypt, 'cept there ain't no pyramids."

"I think it North Africa," said Pook. "Lotta desert there."

"So?" asked Dante. "Where you figure it is, Radgi?"

Radgi shrugged. "I just thought it would be red in a desert."

"Red?"

"I know what he sayin'," said Pook. "I seen pitchers of deserts the color he talkin'. Not red like blood, but more like rust."

Dante nodded. "Oh, yeah. I seen them pitchers, too. In our world geography book. I think there red deserts in Australia."

Radgi shifted on the couch, looking almost sad for a second. "Um, it's cool watching this with you brothers, Dante. But, you think I can take a bath? Like you said?"

Dante smiled, feeling good to be able to show that he cared, like a real Rasta. "Oh, sure, man. Bathroom up the hall on the left, past the kitchen. There some Mr. Bubble on a shelf over the tub."

Radgi's expression changed to a smile. "I never thought homeboys took bubble baths."

Dante turned to give Pook a warning frown, then shrugged. "Well, it save a lotta scrubbin'. Even my dad get down with Mr. Bubble when he come out *Bantu*'s engine room all dirty."

"Thanks, Dante."

Radgi's little brown hand touched Dante's black arm for an instant, and again Dante felt that small sensation of something more than just simple warmth. It was almost the same feeling he got when his father touched him . . . or, he realized, when Pook had put his arm around him earlier. He watched Radgi get clumsily to his feet and take his jacket along.

Pook had been watching too. He waited for the sound of the bathroom door closing, then tapped Dante's leg. "Yo. I still say he sick, man. Look like it hurt him a little to move."

"So, what you figure the matter with him?"

"I don't know, but I gots a feelin' it serious. He should go to a hospital."

Dante snagged the bottle and took a long gulp. "Well, *I* should go to a hospital, but this be Babylon an' the hospital want green. Lots of it. You figure there anythin' in your doctor book might say what wrong with him?"

"Mmm. I check it out."

Dante thought a moment. "You figure *he* know somethin' wrong?"

Pook shrugged in the clumsy way of drunk kids. "Trouble is, if somethin' been wrong a long time, it get to feel normal."

"Guess you could say that about Babylon too." Dante took another swallow from the almost empty bottle and passed it back to Pook. "Here, man, kill this an' we crib."

"Oh, sure." Pook took the bottle and gulped down the last two inches of malt, then slumped back with a sigh and patted his stomach. "So, what we gonna do 'bout that coke, Dante?"

Dante felt a twinge of guilt, as if reminded of an overdue schoolwork assignment. "Funny. I almost forgot about it. Hell, ain't nuthin' we can do tonight. It still be there tomorrow."

Pook considered that, running a hand down his body as if it were numb and he was trying to feel it. Finally, he nodded. "Guess you right, Dante. But what we gonna tell Wyatt in the mornin'?"

"Hell, Pook, don't trip, okay? Maybe Wyatt down there right now doin' some thinkin' of his own. Yo, we all come from too far back in the day to let money bust up the mix." Dante put his arm over Pook's broad shoulder. "Yo, man, why don't you go on to bed. I snag some blankets for Radgi."

Pook lurched to his feet but fell back on the couch. "Whoa," he chuckled. "I think I kinda buzzed."

Dante grinned. "Is that a medical term? Wait, I help ya." He got cautiously to his own feet, then slipped his hands under the other boy's arms. "Ready, man? Go for it!"

Pook was a lot heavier than Dante expected, but he managed to help him upright. They swayed in an awkward embrace for a minute, arms around each other. In a way it felt good to be touching like this, and yet somehow something was missing. Pook stayed slumped against him, arms draped over Dante's shoulders, chest to chest, their foreheads touching, each breathing malt fumes into one another's faces. Dante felt a warmth spread through him, and a sort of protective longing that shaded to sadness because even here, safe at home and holding his friend, he could still feel lonely. Pook's heart beat solid and strong only inches from his own, and yet—though it seemed a strange thing to think—could never *touch* his. Dante murmured unashamed, "I love you, brutha."

Pook smiled. "I love you, too, brutha." Then he broke away and headed up the hall.

Dante stood for a moment, watching him go, the warmth of their closeness still lingering. Then he picked up and thumbed the remote to kill the TV. He went to the linen closet, got two blankets and a pillow, and laid them on the couch. Leaving the lamp on, he walked up the hall. Passing the bathroom, he heard the friendly sound of water splashing into the tub. Wisps of steam curled out from around the door frame, scented by Mr. Bubble. Dante smiled, feeling less lonely now for some reason.

Dante's room was on the house's front corner. The cupola stuck out over a truck yard below like the turret of a castle. Its floor was about two feet higher than the room's, and Dante's bed was a double-sized mattress that just fit the space. The walls were decorated with posters of reggae groups and singers, including Burning Spear and Bob and Ziggy Marley. There were pictures of ships and tugboats, most taken for

Dante by Wyatt, along with many more of all three boys from the time they could toddle, to Pook's birthday party in the café kitchen just weeks before. There was also a sort of collage by some of the best taggers in West Oakland, including Wyatt, with several gang tags; one by a fisherman's son who'd belonged to a low-pro Vietnamese gang. He'd been about eleven, and might have become part of Dante's posse if he hadn't had his throat cut the summer before.

Pook sat on the bed, thumbing through his medical book in the glare of the turret's bare bulb. He had stripped to his boxers, and the sharp shadows cast by the light seemed to further define every hard muscle. The old book looked like a Bible, but bigger. Clad in worn black leather, its tarnished silver title was *The Modern Physician's Advisor,* and its copyright date was 1912. Pook's strong fingers carefully turned the delicate age-yellowed pages.

Dante unbuttoned his jeans and kicked them off into a corner. "Find anythin', Pook?"

Pook shook his head, bent over the book like a young panther doing his homework. "Naw. There somethin' in here 'bout peritonitis, but I don't figure Radgi got that."

Dante yawned and stretched. "My favorite part the chapter 'bout 'the dangers of self-abuse.' Them ole-time people really had 'em some wacked-out ideas."

Pook looked up and smiled. "Oh, sure. But I like the chapter on neurology, where it say us black folk got nuthin' but monkey brains. Course, there wasn't very many black doctors back in them days."

Dante brushed back his dreds. "Hell, I didn't even think they let us be doctors back then."

Pook yawned. "Black doctors for black folks. The only white doctors we could have was veterinarians. They prob'ly diagnose Radgi with myxomatosis."

"The hell?"

Pook smiled again. "It a animal disease."

"Well, you figure that ole book any good for what go wrong with people today?"

"Oh, sure, man. There still a lotta stuff in here a doctor got to know. An' prob'ly a whole lot they don't even teach 'em today. This tell you how to set broken bones, an' put eyes back in, an' deliver babies at home."

"Too bad it don't got a chapter on heart surgery at home."

Pook looked up again. "You sayin' you let me try it?"

"Maybe after another forty. But I hope you can find somethin' to help Radgi. I kinda like that kid."

"Yeah, Dante, so do I."

Dante moved to the full-length mirror mounted on the closet door and studied himself. Maybe it was only the malt, but he wasn't sure that he liked the ebony boy in the glass. The face, he supposed, was okay, and his small muscled body had lots of definition . . . trouble was, there wasn't much there to define. He flexed an arm and frowned at the baby bicep, then noted that all the malt he'd drunk had given him a prominent little-kid's tummy. At best he resembled a wild Bantu boy.

Then his eyes flicked self-consciously to see if Pook had been watching, but Pook was still bent over the book. Dante turned from the mirror.

"Um, Pook? Didn't they used to figure bein' a homo was some sorta disease?"

Pook looked up again. "Lotta people still do."

"Well, yeah. But, I talkin' back then."

"Oh, sure. Whole chapter on that in here."

"So, what s'posed to be the cure?"

Pook studied Dante a moment, then seemed to deliberately look away. "'Wholesome an' manly thoughts an' activities.'" He hesitated, scanning Dante now as if recalling their closeness out in the living room, then seemed to force a casual shrug. "I used to read that chapter a lot."

"Guess it pretty wack, huh?"

This time Pook's shrug was more natural. "All I sayin' is, it didn't work for me."

Dante wasn't sure if it was sadness he felt, or something lonelier. Pook had lowered his eyes back to the book, and his wide shoulders seemed to slump. Dante almost went over to sit beside him, but then wondered what good that would do . . . their hearts could never touch.

"I'ma go piss, man." He left the room and went back up the hall and opened the bathroom door. Radgi stared from the tub, half-buried by bubbles.

"Oh!"

Dante had almost forgotten the kid. He blinked in the brightness of the overhead bulb, catching only a glimpse of Radgi's chubby brown chest before he sank up to his neck in the bubbles.

"Sorry, man. Didn't mean to freak ya. Just gotta piss, is all."

The toilet was right next to the tub. Dante smiled coming over, seeing that Radgi still wore his cap. Dante stepped to the toilet, noting that Radgi's eyes, now even greener in the glare, seemed to scan him with something like interest. As he had at the school fence that day, Dante felt an urge to puff out his pecs no matter how lame that would look. Then, a new thought came, one that he'd never considered before, but now wondered why he hadn't.

"Um, Radgi . . . *you* ain't gay . . . are you?"

Radgi looked slightly surprised, then a funny little smile flickered on his face. "I don't think so."

Dante felt his cheeks warming. Finished, and feeling a fool, he dropped the toilet lid and sat down. He studied the boy in the tub, still up to his neck in the bubbles, his brilliant brown skin tone a beautiful contrast to the bright frothy white. Dante felt somehow protective again. "Um, sorry, man."

Radgi watched a bubble rise and float through the air. "It's cool. I suppose it's a natural kinda question." He considered a moment, then added, "I didn't always live on the street."

Dante smiled too. Radgi's face was clean for the first time he'd seen him, and the small bridge of freckles across his wide nose made him look somehow childish and fierce at the same time. A *rugged child*, Pook had said, meaning a tugboat, but it tagged Radgi too. Then Dante's smile faded. "Um, I . . . guess you had to do a lotta stuff out there on the street? For money, what I sayin'."

Radgi looked away. "Yeah."

"Well, it ain't like that here. Not with me. It ain't the reason I axed you to stay here tonight. Know what I sayin'?"

Was that relief he saw in Radgi's eyes? Dante couldn't be sure, but he hoped so. "What I sayin' is, you *safe* here, man. Don't gotta front. Just be your own self, okay?"

Once more, Radgi smiled that funny little smile. "Okay, Dante. An' thanks. Um, I'm gonna finish my bath now."

"Oh. Sure." Dante got to his feet. He wondered what Radgi was thinking of him . . . homeys with a homo! "Um, see you in the mornin', man."

Pook was in bed, still paging through his book. Dante slipped under the covers beside him.

"Find anythin', Pook?"

"Maybe worms."

Dante groaned. "Aw, hell! Not worms again!"

"Oh, sure. All kinda worms, man . . . roundworms, flatworms, pinworms, tapeworms . . ."

"That *gross*, man! How in hell a kid get fulla worms?"

"Garbage eatin', mostly. Some kinda worm infestations can swell up your stomach."

"Yo! I go wack if I know somethin' alive inside me!"

Pook flipped to the index in the back of the book. Night breeze off the Bay sighed around the turret, its cold breath sifting in past the old window frames. Dante shivered and drew the blankets tighter, wondering what it would be like to face this night alone with only cardboard for covers.

"Pook? What you figure them pigs done to Air Touch? Like a doctor's opinion?"

Pook lay back, setting the book on his chest, his side of the blankets pushed down to his waist. "Mmm. Bruises, lacerations, contusions, possible fractured ribs, maybe a concussion. Could be internal injuries too."

"But, you figure he gonna live, what I axin'?"

Pook shrugged. "Well, them pigs know what to hit an' how hard to hit it. Plenty of practice. Axe me, Air Touch ain't gonna be cruisin' for a few days, but we be seein' him again." He gave Dante a glance. "Y'all *sure* he didn't see you?"

"Yeah."

"Well, that real good, 'cause he gotta be into somebody a way lotta money right now."

Dante cast an uneasy glance at his underwear drawer. "We cool, man. He can't be figurin' nuthin' else but them cops jack the coke and his gun."

Dante heard the bathroom door open and then the soft padding of Radgi's bare feet heading down the hall to the living room. Pook had picked up the book again. He ran a finger down the index, then flipped through the pages, finally opening the book and standing it on Dante's chest.

"I *knowed* I seen him somewheres before."

Dante stared. The book was open at a double-page illustration, the kind called an engraving instead of an actual photo. It was titled *The Family of Man*, and supposedly showed all the races of the world . . . except that the white man in the middle seemed to be up on a pedestal and looked like a god surveying some doubtful creations. All of the figures were male and young, most only looking like boys except for the white man, whose face had mature features as if he did all the thinking. All were naked but for the white, who might have been wearing a 1912 jockstrap. There was an "Asiatic" boy, slit-eyed and skinny, an "Esquamoix," stocky and squinting, an "American Indian," who seemed more embarrassed than anything else, an "East Indian," who looked like a dark-eyed boy-toy, a "Semite," with a huge hooked nose, a burly but brainless-looking "Polynesian," and an "African," who seemed like a cross between John Henry and a lowland gorilla. Only the white man looked like he might have an IQ over forty. The boys down below seemed about ready to start the first multicultural gang fight in history. But Dante's eyes were locked on a last little figure.

It looked a lot like Radgi! Take away his huge tummy and soft chubby chest and that was the boy in Dante's bathtub! Dante could even imagine the backward-turned X cap clamped on that wild bush of hair. Beneath the boy's feet was the tag AUSTRALIAN ABORIGINE.

"The hell!" muttered Dante. "But, how he get *here?*"

Pook closed the book and set it on the windowsill. "Well, Africans ain't the only black people in the world."

"Well, yeah. But I never knew 'bout no others bein' brought here for slaves."

Pook smiled. "So, who sayin' Radgi's people come here like that? This ain't 1912 no more, an' even black folks can travel. Yo. Y'all see some African-lookin' brutha on the street, you don't right away go figure he just off a boat from Rwanda."

"Mmm. Yeah. I see what you sayin'." Dante thought a moment. "So, I guess Wyatt was right today, huh?"

Pook gave Dante a considering look. "Wyatt be right about a lotta stuff, man."

"You been thinkin', huh? I thought you was drunk."

Pook yawned. "I am. That why my thinkin' goin' nowhere. Maybe we do some more in the mornin'."

"Yeah. In the mornin'." Dante reached for the overhead string and clicked off the light. The purple-edged glow of a street lamp seeped in through the grimy window glass. Pook lay back and pulled the blankets up to his chin.

"'Night, Dante."

"'Night, Pook."

7

"Yo, Dante! I still can't believe you left some little hood-rat alone in your apartment!" puffed Wyatt as the boys climbed the stairs to history class.

Dante scowled. "Don't be taggin' somebody you don't even know!"

Wyatt paused, halfway up the staircase. "Okay, man. But don't y'all come cryin' to me if you get home tonight an' he gone, 'long with all the 'mergency money your dad leave for you!"

"Damnit, Wyatt! I told you he ain't feelin' good!"

Wyatt shrugged. "Well, you ain't lookin' too all that yourself today, man." He gave Pook a glance. "An', I can't believe *you* let this fool piss away ten bucks on malt . . . *doctor!*" He searched Dante's eyes, then sighed. "You coulda come down an' told me you wanted a beer."

Pook smiled slightly. "It a little hard to go axin' somebody for somethin' nice right after you pull a gun on 'em."

Dante blew air. "I didn't *mean* to, damnit! It just *happen!*"

Wyatt nodded. "Yeah. I know, man. It cool." He smiled. "Just wish I'd had my camera." He glanced at the stairwell clock. "We can talk about that other stuff later, but . . . an' don't go off again . . . you *sure* you stash the gun an' them packages where Radgi couldn't just 'accidently' find 'em?"

"We stuck it all underneath the sack in the kitchen garbage can."

Pook gave Dante a nudge. "Yo, brutha, I think you gots your shirt on backward again."

"Huh?" Dante looked around to see Shara and her homegirl coming down the stairs. He smiled. "Yo, Shara."

Shara was dressed today in loose jeans and a tank top. Her big breasts swayed as she walked, and their plump roundness showed from the sides of her shirt. Dante tried to keep his eyes on her face and spit game. "Um . . . you really lookin' good today."

But Shara just gave him an icy-edged glance, while nodding warmly enough to the other boys. "Hi, Pook . . . Wyatt." She passed Dante by as if he smelled bad, but then paused two steps down and looked back.

"So, crack what really been wrong with you, Dante. Waste *my* time on no rehab boys!" She turned and went on down the stairs, her homegirl following with a high-toned sniff.

"Wemarkabo," murmured Wyatt.

Dante stared after Shara, openmouthed for a moment, then slammed his fist on the banister. "The *cow!*"

Pook shrugged. "Girls can be fools too, man."

Wyatt snickered. "So can homos."

Kelly and Jinx were already at their desks, Jinx in his usual ragged mesh tee that revealed his sad sloppy shape. His dirty jeans were partly unbuttoned beneath his flabby stomach, and bared half his soot-colored butt, showing he didn't wear shorts. One big battered Con was untied. He smelled like unwashed boy, and his shaggy Afro shadowed his eyes. A licorice stick dangled from his lips as he gazed dully into space. Pook, Dante, and Wyatt took their seats as the bell rang and Mrs. Tyehimba came in. Wyatt leaned over and tapped Dante's head with a pencil. Dante blew air, then pulled a licorice stick from his pack and stuck it in his mouth before turning to Jinx. "Yo. Can I come with you to rehab today?"

At first it seemed like Jinx couldn't comprehend. He stared

at Dante and murmured a wondering, "Zuh?" But then his face went so grateful, it made Dante feel sick. "Sure!"

Mrs. Tyehimba turned from the chalkboard. "Dante? Have you something to share with the class today?"

"Um," said Dante, feeling his face flush as other kids swung around to give him various looks. "I was just axin' if Jinx take me with him to rehab."

Snickers broke out in the room, but Mrs. Tyehimba ignored them. "It's wonderful to see young black men helping each other in crisis. If there were more examples of this kind of support, you would all be reading a completely different history book today . . . one in which we as a people play a much greater role in the shaping of world events and our own destinies, a world in which we have many more choices. . . . As a reminder, we should write a short composition on this theme. Three pages. Due Monday."

The snickers and grins changed to groaning and scowls, and a lot of hard looks were aimed at Dante. The dealer-boy in the front row flipped him a finger and mouthed the word "bitch." Mrs. Tyehimba turned back to the chalkboard. "Please pass in your homework assignments, then open your books to page 266."

The snap of binder rings and the rustle of paper sounded all over the room. Jinx passed his homework to the girl in front of him, and Kelly gave his to the boy in his row. Dante and Pook glanced at each other. Wyatt whacked Dante on the head with his pencil again.

"*Here*, fool! Pass mine up! The hell yours?"

Dante took Wyatt's two sheets of paper. "We didn't do ours."

"*WE?*" Wyatt shot Pook a look. "Aw, maaan, you wackin' too?"

"Wyatt? Do *you* have something you'd like to share with the class?"

"Nuthin' that ain't scatological."

Snickers again rippled the room, and Mrs. Tyehimba frowned. "Wyatt. Your considerable knowledge of natural history would be much more beneficial to you in health, science, and sex-education class. And I'm surprised that you seem to find something funny about Jinx's and Dante's addiction to crack cocaine."

She turned once more to the board. Dante gave Wyatt a furious glare, hissing, "Why don't you just go an' spit it all over the PA system, ass-wipe! Hell, tag it on the wall by the goddamn front door!"

"Uh," came Jinx's whisper. "You gotta do your homework, Dante. They tell you that in rehab. It part of devourin' the self-instructive black child."

"... *What?*" Dante stared at Jinx for a second, then saw Mrs. Tyehimba glaring. "... Oh." He slumped back in his seat and tore off a piece of licorice with his teeth. "Um, yeah. I'ma try an' 'member that, man ... whatever you said. Thanks."

"Uh, you don't look so good today, Dante."

Dante sighed and rolled his eyes. "Tell me 'bout it." Then he opened his book and stared at the page. He found himself wondering how Radgi was. He pictured the chubby brown boy as he and Pook had left him that morning: bundled in blankets on the couch with morning cartoons for company. Dante propped his chin in his hands. At least he wouldn't be thinking about Shara anymore! *The cow!* He found that he could picture her full-figured form but, strangely, not much of her face. He scanned the room, letting his eyes linger on other female shapes and feeling the familiar frustration of trying to imagine them willingly surrendering their secrets to his eager embrace. Finally, he sighed again and forced his mind to South African politics. Girls were like BART trains, one of the cool posers had said: be another one along in a few minutes. And he had a lot more choices than Pook.

A folded-up note landed on his desktop. Eyeing the teacher's back, he opened it to see Kelly's squared pencil print: WORD OUT ON .357, KID. GOT CAPS?

Dante gave the Korean boy a nod, then, still watching Mrs. Tyehimba, he leaned over and passed Pook the apartment keys. "Yo," he whispered. "Tell Radgi I hope he be feelin' better."

After class, Dante waited in the ground-floor hallway with Jinx, who had said that another rehab kid would be joining them. It seemed strange to see Pook and Wyatt leaving without him. He couldn't recall many times when they all hadn't hung together after school. A few of the other kids passing eyed Dante and Jinx with a mix of expressions. One of a trio of seniors paused and dropped his pants. "Yo, shitheads! Here some crack you can suck!"

Dante turned to Jinx as the big boys strutted off laughing. "How you cope with the dissin', man?"

"Zuh? Oh. Uh . . ." Jinx shrugged. His jeans sagged under his soft sack of stomach, and his loose shoelace trailed on the floor. "Nobody never like me anyways."

"Well . . . *why?* What I sayin' is, there nuthin' really wrong with you."

Jinx only looked confused, his hands hanging limp at his sides, his posture like a potbellied question mark. "Uh, there musta been . . . 'cept, I can't 'member what it was." Then he brightened a little and added, "Least I know what wrong with me now: I self-disruptive."

". . . Um. Yeah." Dante glanced at the clock above the front doors. "I gotta see a man 'bout a dog. Back in a minute."

The bathroom seemed to be empty, echoing as the door shut behind him. The overhead fluorescents reflected from wall and floor tiles the color Wyatt called baby-poo green. The air was still hazy with dope and tobacco smoke and the sweetish chemical traces of crack. Dante came around the partition and saw the dealer-boy from history class at the urinal. The kid was about his own size, but skinny. He was sucking a blunt that had been soaked in malt liquor . . . though Dante had never been able to figure the logic in that. Dante ignored him, stepping up to the trough and unzipping his jeans. The kid gave him a glare but then seemed to reconsider. He buttoned his baggies, then leaned against the wall.

"Yo, Dante, nobody make it in rehab. Just peep Jinx . . . suckin' on licorice, everybody crackin' his ass. You never stop wantin' it, y'know? You always be thinkin' 'bout how *good* it feel."

Dante shrugged. "Kinda like love, ain't it?"

"Huh?" The kid frowned a moment, then spread his hands. "Yo, fool, the party ain't even started yet! So, when you decide you gonna quit? Yesterday?" He smirked. "Ole Miz T's little speech make y'all feel pretty good, huh? *Yesterday.* But, y'all ain't lookin' too fly *today*, man. An', trust me, G, it *really* gonna hurt tomorrow!" He nodded knowingly. "An', all the time it hurtin', the suckas gonna be dissin' your tender little ass! They never let you forget what you are!" He flipped the blunt into the urinal to show he could afford to.

Dante zipped his jeans as the boy spit on the floor and started to leave. "Yo. What your name?":

The boy stopped. "Huh?"

"You *do* gots one, don't ya?"

The boy gave Dante an uncertain look that shaded into suspicion, but then shrugged. "Bam-Bam. Everbody know." He searched Dante's face for a reaction. "'Cause of Bed-*rock*, know what I sayin'?"

". . . Oh. Yeah . . . cool." Dante thought fast. Meeting Bam-Bam in here had been an accident. He hadn't thought much about what he could do with Air Touch's coke, but now was a lucky chance to take a snoop. Everybody knew how to score, but nobody but a slick-boy would ask where the shit came from. Bam-Bam would be at the bottom of the house-nigger food chain, but you had to start somewhere. Dante offered a down-with-it smile.

"So, Bam-Bam, you deal anythin' 'sides rock?"

Suspicion flickered again on the other boy's face as pride went against wariness. He checked Dante's eyes: still dull from

drinking and too little sleep. Finally he came a casual pose, leaning against a toilet stall. "Yo, I gots *anythin'* anybody need, man!"
Then he smiled. "Yo, Rastamon, got some sweet island herb. Get
you closer to Jah."

Dante took a thoughtful stance. "Uh-huh. But, how 'bout
somethin' hit, man? An', I ain't talkin' 'bout that cut-down concrete candy Air Touch sell."

Bam-Bam smirked. "You a G who all that. Funny I read you
wrong all this time." Then he gave Dante a considering look. "I
won't be dealin' with Air Touch no more. Boy tell me he movin'
up, got business goin' on, know what I sayin'? Fact is, I just
might be takin' his place." He studied Dante again. "So, what on
your mind, man? You talkin' scratch-an'-sniff, or poke-an'-pop?"

Dante tapped his nose with a fingertip, almost amazed to dis-
cover how easy it was to lie to a liar. "What it is, there was this white
boy used to come cruisin' the docks. But he just been busted."

"Ooooo," said Bam-Bam, as if that explained everything.
"Yeah. A white boy. Don't that just figure? Everybody know
they gots the slamminest shit." He looked almost wistful a
moment. "Wish I had me a hookup like that. Suckas be
creamin' their jeans when *my* Viper come bumpin'!"

Dante shrugged. "Well, I don't figure my whitey gonna be
sidelined *too* long. Know what I sayin'?"

"Yeah. Tell me 'bout it, man! Pigs pop *my* ass, first time, I
doin' five years!" Bam-Bam spit on the floor again. "So, what he
get, man . . . six months' pro?"

"Um, two months' community service."

Bam-Bam shook his head. "Ain't no justice!" Then he spread
his hands again. "Look, Dante, I sorry 'bout flippin' y'all, okay?
An', I ain't gonna front. I can't get what you want, man . . . not
yet, anyhow. Maybe later when Air Touch move up." Bam-Bam
smiled a little. "Yo, man. This for free, G to G. Cruise your black
ass up to that park on Broadway. Come correct so Five-o scan

you a high-top Afro-American. Maybe you hook another whitey till your own boy back with the pack."

Bam-Bam turned to leave, but grinned over his shoulder. "Just beep me it happen, okay?" He pointed. "My number right there on the wall."

Dante grinned in return and flashed a peace sign. Bam-Bam pushed past Jinx, who had just come in.

"The fuck out my way, licorice-breath!"

The other boy let himself be shoved aside. "Uh, Dante? We ready to go."

Bam-Bam's laughter echoed back from the hallway: "Rehab, my ass!"

Dante glared at Jinx. "Pull up them stupid pants, fool!"

"Zuh?"

"Hell!" Dante grabbed the top of Jinx's jeans and yanked them up. He managed to get one more button fastened under the boy's stomach, then dropped to a crouch and tied Jinx's shoelace. Jinx gave him another wondering look. "Uh . . . thanks, man."

"Zuh," Dante muttered.

He was surprised to find that the other kid waiting outside was a girl. She was about his own age, deep dusky brown, and looked pretty in braids, black Paris sweatshirt and Ben Davis baggies. The shapes of her breasts beneath the big shirt were well-formed and full. Her waist was probably narrow, though the shirt hid her figure, but her hips and bottom filled out her jeans. Her face was . . . interesting: childlike but betrayed by a slowness to alter expression. It could have been cute in the glow of a candle, but the hallway's harsh glare showed suggestions of lines where there shouldn't have been. Her eyes had that faint smoky haze of lightbulbs after a long power surge, and the skin below them looked slightly smudged. Still, her smile was wide and more friendly than not, though somehow a little too foxy.

"This Jasmine," said Jinx. "Jasmine, this Dante."

Jasmine met Dante's eyes for a moment. There was a hint of calculation in her look, but it seemed more like an automatic response than judgment. Her smile warmed as if drawing power from an unseen source. Dante felt her eyes going over him and maybe it was interest that brightened them.

"Hi, Dante. I seen you around. I got PE the same period."

"Um, oh." Dante had almost tried to harden his chest just a little, but realized that Jasmine would have seen him shirtless alongside Pook, so what was the point?

But there was no trace of mocking in her smile or her tone. "I wondered what was wrong with you. I mean, everybody know about Pook."

"Uh, Dante gots a bad heart," explained Jinx, and Dante could have kicked him.

"It 'cause of crack," said Dante. "My mom was on it."

Jasmine looked sad. "They told us about that in rehab. It made you be born afflictively-declined."

". . . Huh?"

"Jasmine got entirely dis-enflowered when she was twelve," Jinx announced. "By a pimp."

". . . *What?*" Dante frowned. "Ain't no reason to go tellin' stuff like that, man."

Jinx only shrugged. "Well, everbody gots to tell on each other in rehab. It part of the abortive peer-group sterilization an' disenfranchisement process."

Dante sighed. "Oh, cool."

The rehab center was a small shabby storefront, the glass of its street-facing windows blanked with green paint so the afternoon sun gave the inside an emerald glow, like being in an aquarium. Dante hadn't known what to expect, maybe something like a medical clinic, but was somehow disappointed to find that the place looked mostly like the extinct little neighborhood drug and variety shop it was. The floor was cracked and curling asphalt tile, a dusty beige color and showing the ghosts where racks and counters had stood. The smudged plaster walls were scarred with screw holes where shelves had once been, and scabby with yellowed old strips of Scotch tape that had held advertisements. Part of a sign for skin lightener still hung curled in a corner. There were a few anti-drug/alcohol/gang/tobacco/violence posters stuck here and there, but no different from those in the hallways at school. A big cork-board on the back wall was plastered with thumbtacked notes, most childishly printed in pencil, and a few faded pictures of kids. The only furniture was a dozen old folding chairs in two ragged rows that faced a battered wooden lectern at the rear of the room, and in one back corner a table near a closed door. On the table were plain paper cups, a stainless-steel pitcher, and a flyspecked jar of licorice sticks. The air was stuffy and hot, smelling of dry rot and dust and the sweaty-kid scent of a classroom.

There were six other kids in the place: four boys and two girls. Five sprawled or sat slumped in the chairs while the sixth, a thin, hollow-cheeked boy of eleven or twelve, stood at the corkboard scoping the notes. The girls sat together, murmuring low, but the boys were scattered all over and mostly ignored each other. Some sucked on licorice. Dante got the feeling of glances turned briefly to him as he entered behind Jinx and Jasmine, but didn't sense much of a welcome. A few yo's and s'ups were exchanged, but more automatic than anything else. A little while ago Dante would have tagged Jinx as being about as live as library paste, but here he looked like the most happenin' B in the house.

Jinx went over to talk with one of the boys. Jasmine gave Dante a smile that seemed a little mysterious before joining the girls. Left alone, Dante scanned the room, looking for a clock, but there wasn't one. He noticed that most of the kids had shed backpacks beneath their chairs, so he set his down beside Jinx, then walked over to study the corkboard. The thin boy, mud-brown and lost in a big loose athletic tank top, gave him an uncertain smile and edged out of his way. The messages, Dante saw, were mostly kid-to-kid, and generally set up places and times to meet. One or two sounded suspiciously like offers or threats from dealers. There were several from parents, all pleas to come home, and the notes beneath every picture began with the ominous word "missing." There were a few handbills: one for a youth shelter, another for County Counseling Services, two for abortion clinics, two that appealed to "have your baby because someone is waiting to love it," an old one for DARE, and another from The Boys and Girls Club, "The club that beats the streets." McGruff the Crime Dog advised kids to join his gang before joining someone else's. Three more, all with fringes of phone numbers on the bottom, seemed to be from people who wanted "young models" for "art" or "photography." One "desired" boys and girls between the ages of eight and eighteen. Another wanted only boys of the same ages, while the last specified "muscular African-American boys 13–15, seeking big money and excitement." Thinking of Pook and smiling faintly, Dante walked over to the table.

He glanced at the licorice and wrinkled his nose. The pitcher seemed to be full of cockroach-colored Kool-Aid. He poured half a paper cupful and gave it a tentative taste. It might have been grape, but was weak and warm, not sugared enough, and wouldn't even have mixed up a decent chicken-bottle. He glanced over his shoulder, noted that no one was watching, and poured the rest of it back in the pitcher before crumpling the cup and dropping it into a rusty wastebasket under the table. He was about to give the corkboard another peep when he heard heavy footsteps approaching from the other side of the door. A quick scan of the other kids showed them taking about the same poses as when a teacher came into a classroom. The thin boy hurried to a chair, and Dante came back to take a seat between Jinx and Jasmine. Jasmine gave him a smile that was both sly and almost amused, while Jinx seemed slightly nervous. The door creaked open on unoiled hinges and a big fat white woman entered.

She looked like a girls' prison guard, and her smile was about as welcoming as a knife slash with teeth. She carried a wrinkled file folder that bulged with paper, and plopped it down on the lectern while scanning the kids in the room. Her eyes passed Dante twice, then she shuffled through the folder and finally looked him a question. Dante wasn't sure who should speak first. He met the big woman's gaze and felt resentment rising inside him because it seemed as if she was deliberately trying to stare him down. Only seconds passed but they seemed like hours, and Dante had a silly thought that this might go on for the whole rehab session. From the corner of his eye he noted the other kids watching, some only bored but others seeming expectant as if sharing a secret joke. Jinx shifted uneasily in his seat, but Jasmine was just smiling her sly smile again.

Finally, Jinx cleared his throat and stood up. "Uh, this my friend Dante, Miz Conrad. He a socially-emphatic subsistence-afflicted black kid, like me."

Dante thought the woman looked pissed, but maybe a little grateful that Jinx had broken the standoff. Her eyes shifted focus, still on Dante, but studying him now.

"Thank you, Jinx. But, the next time you bring a sociopathic substance-addicted minority youth among us, remember to tell him our rules."

"Oh, yeah," said Jinx. "Uh, Dante, you got to go up an' reduce yourself to the peer abort-group."

"*Introduce* yourself to *your peer-support* group," said the woman.

"Zuh? But I already done that a long time ago."

The woman scowled. "It's *his* peer-support group too."

". . . Oh."

The woman sighed and beckoned to Dante. "Come here."

Though the shabby setting was similar to a schoolroom, Dante was surprised to hear none of the usual snickers of see smirks as he rose and walked up to face the crew. Traffic-sound carried from out on the street, but in here just the squeak of his Nikes seemed loud. The big woman stayed behind the lectern and offered no sign of support. Dante felt a lot like he did when having to do an oral book report when he hadn't read the book, but he thought he sensed sympathy in most of the other kids' eyes . . . maybe more in Jinx's and Jasmine's.

"Um, my name's Dante."

Silence. Jinx looked miserable now; Jasmine still amused. Seconds crawled. At last, Dante turned to the woman. "Well?"

She frowned, first at Dante, then at Jinx, but finally sighed again. "Tell us what you are."

"Huh? . . . Well, I be a Rasta. Why I wearin' these dreds."

Now a few snickers did slip out of the other kids. Dante felt sweat sheening his forehead. Then he saw Jinx mouthing words, and struggled to read the boy's lips.

". . . Oh. I a . . . socially-active, self-instructive . . ."

"You are a sociopathic, self-destructive, drug-abusing young African-American male!" snapped the woman.

"Oh, sure," said Dante.

Seven smiles came on automatically. The eighth, Jasmine's, was more of a sympathetic smirk. Eight voices responded like a tired church choir. "Hiiii, Dante."

The woman came around to Dante's side, her slashlike smile more approving now. "Hello, Dante. My name is Ms. Conrad, and we all welcome you to your state-sponsored, behavioral-stabilization, self-image-enhancement and socioeconomic empowerment program. Your supportive peer-group will now introduce themselves."

Jinx was the first on his feet like a flabby little robot. He seemed to have gone from miserable to terminally shy. "Uh, my name's Jinx, an' I a crack-cocaine-inflicted young Afro-'merican male."

Then came Jasmine, still slightly smirking, and then, one by one, the other kids, rising to their feel like reluctant zombies to tell Dante their names and babble their shames. It was awful.

Dante had expected to have to tell on himself, and improvised the usual crap about being poor and having no hope in a Babylon that hated black kids and was doing everything possible to prove it. Behind him he could hear the scratch of Ms. Conrad's pen as she made notes, but the whole thing sounded terminally boring, even to his own ears. Jinx only nodded, along with most of the other kids who'd probably heard it all before, but Dante thought Jasmine looked skeptical.

Dante didn't know what to expect when he finished — maybe a great big supportive-peer-group hug and a Kool-Aid and licorice party in his honor — but Ms. Conrad only came around from behind the lectern and took hold of his shoulder with one huge pink hand.

"Come with me, Dante. You will now begin the first step toward your socio-chemical rehabilitation."

Maybe it was her Crypt-Keeper tone, or the ghostly smirks he now saw on most of the other kids' faces, but Dante had a bad feeling about this. He looked to Jinx, who wouldn't meet his eyes, then to Jasmine. Her knowing smile wasn't reassuring.

Keeping a firm hold on his shoulder, Ms. Conrad steered Dante toward the door in back, reached ahead of him to open it, then marched him into a hot, stuffy hallway. He remembered old movies about death row and that last lonely walk to eternity. The hall had two closed doors on either side and one at the end that was steel-plated and probably led to an alley, though right then Dante wouldn't have been surprised to find a gas chamber beyond.

But Ms. Conrad stopped him at the first door on the left. It was plain old wood and peeling gray paint; just a door that might lead to a former stockroom. Dante noticed the lock was an ancient skeleton-key type and that a rusty key poked from the hole. Ms. Conrad twisted the knob and pushed the door open. It creaked on old hinges. The room was small and square, about ten feet by ten, its walls and floor of tongue-and-groove board, its ceiling of plaster, all painted pale green. It was windowless and even hotter than the hallway. A single small bulb burned overhead. The only furniture was a straight-backed wooden chair that faced the far wall. Ms. Conrad's voice kept its slight Crypt-Keeper titter: "Sit down in the chair, Dante. The first step in your rehabilitation process will be a period of silent self-assessment and inner-child evaluation. While your testimony suggests that you may have a congenital addictive-inclination, you should nevertheless disregard environmental and racio-socio-economic factors as being justifiable sanction for majori-tal culture estrangement, leading to social disempowerment, which has resulted in chemical dependency." She paused for a breath. "Eventually you will arrive at the conclusion that you are a self-abu-sive failure; *not* a victim of poverty, discrimination, or racism, and of absolutely no value to American society in your present state of self-inflicted dysfunction."

"Zuh?"

"After a suitable period of this solitary self-assessment, and guided by your supportive-peer-group, we will initiate a conse-cution of re-education, through which you will gain nonthreat-ening self-image enhancement, realistically obtainable life-goal objectives, and socially-acceptable minority empowerment."

"Um, maybe I ain't ready to be devoured yet," said Dante.

But the big woman only steered him to the chair and sat him firmly down. "Begin."

Dante had a sudden impulse to run . . . was this old cow crazy? The hell did she figure she was? He spun around in the chair as she walked to the door. He almost leaped to his feet, but he *had* promised Jinx. He was putting up with this shit for Jinx. How bad could it be? At least he wasn't washing Wyatt's dishes!

The door closed. Dante tensed, his eyes going wide as he heard the key turn. The hell was going on here! How could she lock him in! There were supposed to be laws against this sort of thing! He did leap up then, darting to the door and trying the knob. It really *was* locked! That wack-ass old bitch! What if there was a fire? What if he had an attack? What if he had to go to the bathroom? He opened his mouth to yell. Damnit, he wasn't like those other fools out front! He didn't *deserve* being treated like this! But then he blew air and brushed back his dreds. Oh, what the hell, how hard could it be? After all, Jinx had survived.

And look at what he is now!

The heat seemed to double with the door shut: that dead, dry heat of closed-up rooms where mummified flies flat-backed in dust. Sweat ran down Dante's face. His T-shirt was already soaked under the arms and clung to his body. There didn't seem any sense in just standing and sweating. How long could this "self-assessment" session last anyhow . . . maybe an hour? Chill with the flavor. He walked back to the chair and found he was thirsty. Even a cupful of that rat-piss in the pitcher would have gone down good. He stripped off his shirt and sat. Then he discovered that the chair was screwed to the floor so it would only face the far wall. How could this sort of shit "rehabilitate" anybody! Dante scowled and got up. It ragged him to know that he was *supposed* to sit in the chair and nowhere else. To hell with "nonthreatening images"!

Shirt slung over one shoulder, he paced around the walls: five steps, turn, five steps, turn, five steps. . . . One corner near the door seemed coolest, and he finally sank into it on the floor. Faint traffic and city sounds seeped from outside but seemed strangely distant. He wondered what the other kids were talking about in the main room. Maybe *they* were all just sitting there assessing their self-abusive selves until they were ready to believe Babylonian babble? He glanced at the bulb in the ceiling, noting that the fixture was set just enough off center to annoy him somehow. So was the chair, and he was supposed to just sit in it and think about being a "failure"? Well, screw the old cow and her wack-ass rehab! He *wasn't* sitting in her stupid chair, and he sure as shit wasn't going to think about what she'd told him to . . . whatever in hell that was! Anyway, he wasn't a failure: He was only unlucky! Unlucky that his dad had married a woman who couldn't cope with "majorital-culture estrangement" . . . who had gotten her fool self hooked on the white man's poison that had screwed up his heart and finally killed her as she was bringing him into this wack-ass world!

He scowled again, glaring at the opposite corner. This was what the old cow probably wanted him to do! He got up and went to the door. He tried the knob again and pushed at the panel. There was a looseness to the lock, and the door itself wasn't any stronger than an inside door had to be. A few determined lunges might bust it open. . . . But the effort in this heat might also give him an attack. He wondered if it would teach her a lesson if he died self-assessing.

He pictured Pook: One slam of his shoulder would probably rip that old door right off its hinges. Pook, his homo homeboy, his big beautiful knight in bronze-muscled armor coming to his rescue. Then he sighed and returned to the corner. He was doing this for Jinx, even if it was so way past stupid that just the light from the stupid would take ten years to get here!

He fiddled with his sweat-wet shirt for a moment, then tossed it away in a wadded-up ball. He counted the crawling time by chanting, "One empowerment, two empowerment," to space off the seconds, but gave up after minutes started to seem more like hours. Sweat dripped from under his arms and ran down his sides. The crotch of his jeans was wet now too, and the slick heat down there was making him hard.

He cupped himself, his dick eager as a puppy for the stroke of his hand. He glanced at the door. Why not? He was supposed to be self-abusive anyhow, and it would give him something to assess, at least. And, someone to think about.

Who?

He tried to picture Shara, but she wouldn't come clear in his mind anymore. Jasmine? He considered what she might looked like beneath her baggy G-clothes. The shapes of her breasts had been promising. He unbuttoned his jeans. His boxers were soaked with sweat and his ebony shaft couldn't wait to escape its steamy prison. It stood straight and throbbing with empowerment. He gripped it in his hand and a pleasurable shiver ran through him. Okay, he'd self-assess until the cow came back.

Then, outside in the hallway, he heard a soft thunk as if something small had fallen on the floor. He scrambled to his feet, fumbling with his jeans to get them buttoned again as the creak of old hinges sounded outside. He grabbed up his shirt, wondering if it would trip the old bitch that he'd taken it off. To hell with her! He stood there facing the door in defiance . . . and he hadn't stayed in her stupid chair either!

The key turned in the lock. Dante put on his pouty little lion expression. The door opened slowly, and his jaw dropped as Jasmine peeked in.

"Wha—?"

The girl frowned slightly and put a finger to her lips. She slipped quickly inside and eased the door shut behind her, then smiled, her eyes scanning Dante's gleaming black body.

"Shhh, Dante," she whispered. Her smile widened. "Thought you might be gettin' lonely in here."

Dante swallowed. He was thirsty, but his throat was dry now because Jasmine had shed her big T-shirt to reveal a tight white boy's tank top beneath. Her breasts were even more than he'd imagined, robust and round, their big nipples budding the thin cotton cloth. Her dark skin had its own sheen of dampness and shone in the lightbulb's dim glow.

". . . Um, is it over already?" asked Dante. A second ago he'd wanted nothing else than to get out of here, but now he felt reluctant to leave.

Jasmine was eyeing him openly and without any hint of shyness. Dante decided she liked what she saw. Her eyes lowered to the returning bulge in the crotch of his jeans.

"We only been in fifteen minutes. Miz Conrad always lock us down for a hour."

Dante swallowed again. The tank top clung to Jasmine's supple form like a second skin. It was the next-best thing to actually seeing bare breasts . . . bare and *beautiful* breasts! Her waist seemed almost impossibly slim above the lush swells of hips: He imagined he might almost encircle it with his hands.

". . . Um . . . *us?*"

"I was in the room 'cross the hall."

". . . Oh. But, you ain't new here, why you in lockdown?"

Jasmine giggled. "'Behavioral stabilization.' I 'regressed.'" She gave Dante another of those looks that most girls gave Pook when he was shirtless. "On purpose. Want some 'peer-support'?"

Once more Dante swallowed. He told himself to stop coming shy, to look at her body the way she seemed to be looking at his. The desperate word "lust" flashed through his mind. His voice was only a husky rasp now: "But . . . how you get out?"

The girl cocked her head. "Don't y'all never watch no ole spy movies? You take a piece of binder paper an' slide it under the door. Then you push the key out the lock with a hairpin, it fall on the paper, you pull it back under an' let yourself out."

". . . Oh. That, um, that pretty cool."

Jasmine sniffed. "For a girl, what you sayin'."

"Oh, no. For anybody. 'Cept, I don't got no hairpins."

A new thought came, and Dante's dick got harder than ever. He stopped trying to hide it and even reached down to tug at his Ryes to give it more room for expansion. "You sayin' you got yourself locked down on purpose? 'Cause of me?"

Her smile was sly and knowing again. "Well, duh." She took a step nearer to him. "We got us 'bout forty-five minutes. Wanna 'free-associate'?"

". . . Oh." Again, Dante swallowed. Despite his throbbing desire, he felt a slight shiver of fear. In all of his dreams this sort of thing happened, yet the times and the places were always his own. He'd imagined making his first love everywhere from a white sandy beach to a penthouse hotel room, but mostly he'd pictured it happening on his own bed. Somehow, there had always been sheets and softness or the crashing of waves on a seashore included. He glanced around the small room: hot and dusty and pale pukey green. There was nowhere to do it but on those bare boards among dried-out fly corpses. People said you remembered your first time all your life.

Maybe Jasmine saw his uncertainty. She stripped off her tank top and casually stretched. Dante lost every doubt in an instant. Those beautiful breasts! That dark, dusky body! All his to touch . . . *finally!*

He moved to her, hardly daring to believe this was real. He slipped his arms around her, clumsy at first, as if fearing to damage a delicate thing. But the heat in him mounted. He pulled their bodies together, desperate to feel her against him, skin to slick skin, her breasts to his chest, the touch of her nipples to his like tiny tingles of pleasure. It was she who began the kiss, soft lips, searching tongue. He was surprised for a second, his mind and body already flooded with too many new sexual sensations. Part of him wanted everything now, but another small part wished for more time.

The taste of her tongue was both salty and sweet. Dante's chest heaved for breath. He could feel his heart pound, but fiercely, as if it too wanted this thing and would give all its power to have it. Jasmine's hands slid down Dante's sweat-slicked sides to expertly open his jeans. His whole body shook as she gripped him, her hands soft and hot. He almost came then, but strained to hold back. Desperately, he reached for her jeans but she was also ahead of him there.

"I got one," he moaned. "In my wallet."

But she had one already. It seemed to have materialized like magic, and she had him sheathed in a second before he could cool a single degree. It was all beyond his control now, but that didn't matter because he would have done anything to keep this going on. Even Ms. Conrad busting into the room couldn't have stopped him. The floorboards could have been cottony clouds adrift in an ocean of bubbles.

And then it was over, way too soon, leaving him gasping and panting flat on his back on the floor, arms sprawled out, jeans and shorts at his ankles, the boards beneath him slick with his sweat. Grinning like a fool, he watched Jasmine pull up her jeans. Stupidly, he wanted a cigarette. And stupidly he grinned even wider as she pulled a pack of Kools from her pocket and shook up two, kneeling to slip one into his lips, the other into her own, and then firing both with a Bic. He sucked smoke deep, almost coughing, but feeling as if his whole life had been rehabilitated and even the ugly green room looked charming. As if floating in feathery fog, he saw her glance at a cheap plastic watch on her wrist. Then, a little disappointed, he watched her slip into her shirt. She blew smoke and sat down on the chair, facing backward to look down at him. Dante just lay there: If she wanted to scope him, that was kickin'. He felt as if his body was every bit as beautiful and buffed as Pook's.

"I usually get ten dollars."

"... *Huh?*" Dante's eyes widened. He sat up, feeling a splinter jab his bare butt. He suddenly pictured himself and realized that he would have been in about the same pose after spanking his own monkey. For a moment he wondered if he'd heard the girl right.

"... But ... I thought you was off crack?"

Jasmine shrugged. "Figure they give you a prize for that? The world don't change just 'cause you been self-image-entranced an' assertively-sterilized. You still gotta eat." Then she smiled. "You was all that, Dante. You a big, strong brotherman."

Dante glanced down at his small-muscled shape, then blew air. "Uh-huh."

"You can pay me tomorrow if you don't got it now." Jasmine pointed with her cigarette. "I even throw in the hat. They good ones. Extra-strength an' pre-lubricated."

Dante looked down between his legs. The condom felt slimy and cold. He peeled it off, then frowned and flung it away. He jerked the Kool from his mouth and mashed it out on the floor, hearing it hiss in his sweat. "I got ten dollars," he muttered. "The hell, it only a part of acceptin' my realistic life choices!"

"So, Dante? What y'all learn in rehab today?"

Dante sighed. "Before, or after, I got deflowered?"

Wyatt raised an eyebrow. "Huh?"

"Forget it, man."

Dante lay on his back on Wyatt's bed, knees up, one leg over the other, and his arms crossed under his head. His body seemed to want to remember what had happened that afternoon, but his mind could have almost cared less. Like his own, Wyatt and Cheo's room was at the front of the house but had no turreted cupola in the corner. Wyatt's side was mostly decorated with the hundreds of snapshots he'd taken over the years with his little Kodak, photos ranging from Dante and Pook in the bathtub together as little boys, to Kelly Pak's operation with Pook wielding tweezers, to all the posse doing a tag-team hit the week before. There were also animal posters from the zoo, and a lot of smaller pictures cut from the pages of *National Geographic*. The bedspread was fake leopard fur, and the pillowcase striped like a zebra. A big wire cage by the window housed a huge gopher snake that Wyatt had captured three years ago in a junkyard. It lay coiled on pine shavings, which gave off a wild sort of scent.

Dante felt Wyatt's questioning look, so he sighed again and recited, "Crack is a dangerous an' unpredictable drug. It made in a wash process from base cocaine. It was seen by wholesale drug dealers, who are foreign terrorists, as a cheap substitute for real coke, affordable to the less-affluent members of American society, an' a insidious corruption of this nation's beloved minority youth. It be ten times more addictive than cocaine, an' can cause seizures an' heart failure at any time. Babies born to mothers on crack are addicted at birth, an' often suffer from low birth weight, unproperly developed lungs, or defective hearts."

Once more, Dante sighed. "An', it sold mainly to po' niggas, an' whitey want that 'cause it either kill us or screw us up so's he can keep us under control."

Wyatt cocked his head. "They tell you *that* in rehab?"

Dante shrugged. "No. Prob'ly 'cause it the truth."

Wyatt glanced at Cheo, who sprawled on his own bed with Walkman headphones clamped to his ears. He was reading a *Wolverine* comic while munching leftover lasagna. Like Wyatt, he seemed to resent the whole concept of clothes and stripped to his boxers the second he got home to let all his blubber flop around free. His side of the room was hip-hop posters and stickers, and his name had been beautifully tagged on the wall by Wyatt. On his bedside table was a small ant farm, the tiny black creatures eternally busy with what was important in their world and probably never knowing they were part of a bigger one. Cheo was usually cool enough to keep to himself when the older boys were talking.

"Well," said Wyatt, keeping an eye on his little brother. "Don't that make you think any different 'bout what you got stashed upstairs? Like, you helpin' 'em to do it to us, man."

Dante frowned. The truth was that after suffering through that stupid suckhole of a rehab project, then being made all the more miserable by having to pay Jasmine for what should have been a beautiful thing, and *then* having to sit listening to a fat white woman babble on about "socially-acceptable self-images and empowerment for disadvantaged minority youth," with Jinx nodding brainlessly on one side and Jasmine smirking like the Junior Ho-Queen of Babylon on the other, he *did* feel a lot different. *Dirty* would best describe it: a house nigger himself who might be selling everyone down the big river.

What had made the whole thing seem even worse was finding Jinx *knew* what had gone on in that goddamn green room! After rehab was over, Jasmine had left in a different direction, while Dante and Jinx had headed for the nearest bus stop. Sitting on the splintery old bench with their shirts off in the late afternoon sun, Jinx had asked in all innocence, "Uh, was it good for you, Dante?"

At first Dante hadn't been sure he'd heard right, and then for a second he'd figured that Jinx was just asking about the session. Dante had searched the other boy's face for a smirk, but then realized that Jinx probably wasn't capable of slyness. Jinx seemed to accept anything that Babylon shoved in his face as his rightful reward for being one of its "failures." Still, Dante had asked, "You mean, bein' locked in that room?"

"Zuh?" Jinx had looked confused, which seemed to be his only alternate to looking resigned. "No, Dante, I talkin' 'bout you an' Jasmine in there."

Dante had felt something close to horror. "The hell, man! You sayin' *everybody* in that goddamn place know?"

Jinx had still looked confused, and Dante wondered if he'd look that way dead. "Uh, no . . . least, I don't think so, Dante. She never done it in there with nobody else but me."

Dante's mouth had hung open. He'd stared at the other boy almost in wonder and actually felt sick for a second. Slumped on the bench, Jinx looked disgusting; a, soot-colored, marshmallow mess of a kid, so flabby his navel squished shut when he sat and the nipples of his blubbery breasts flattened to soft little slits. Dante wanted to tell him to pull up his pants and put his shirt on. And then a thought came, that in holding Jasmine, kissing her mouth, and doing it there on the floor, he'd somehow been hold-

ing and kissing . . . and fucking . . . Jinx too! He'd stared at the
other boy's lips: loosely open to show big buck teeth with a chip.
He'd almost *felt* his tongue slipping over that chip and Jinx's
sloppy body pressed to his own!

A feeling of fury had mounted in him for a moment, but then
slowly passed, leaving a strange sort of loneliness and then something almost like sympathy. He'd slipped an arm over Jinx's
pudgy shoulders and asked, "Yo, bruthaman, wanna come over
my crib? We can cruise by Kelly's on the way. Kick us a couple
four-o's of Eightball. 'Rehabilitate' our own little sorry-ass selfs."

"Zuh? . . . but, alcohol is a drug too. It can be afflictive an'
promote self-intrusive . . ."

Dante sighed. "Jinx, shut up. Y'all wanna have a goddamn
drink with me or not?"

Something had struggled to light behind Jinx's eyes, like an old
neon sign that wasn't quite dead. "Uh, sure, Dante. That be cool!"

Now, on Wyatt's bed, Dante couldn't remember why he'd felt
good sitting there in the sunlight with Jinx, or why it had seemed
so important to bring the boy home. Maybe it was all Jah's idea?
Dante gave Wyatt a narrow-eyed stare. "Only thing I'ma be sure
of is gettin' that shit sold up where it belong." Dante glanced at
Cheo, but the faint headphones sounds signified that the volume
was cranked. "An,'" he added, "for the green it *really* be worth!"

Wyatt made a face, then waddled his bulk over to another
mesh cage where what might have been the biggest rat in
Oaktown clutched at the wire in eagerness to be fed. It wasn't
white, but a regular rat-colored rodent. Dante watched as Wyatt
opened the door and lifted the animal out, cradling it in one arm
while it gobbled rat food from his hand.

Dante didn't want to talk about rehab anymore, and he hadn't
even told Pook about having sex . . . yet. He wondered a moment
if Jinx, now upstairs, would tell him, but decided he didn't much
care. "Look like Havoc hungry tonight. Where Chaos?"

"Doin' her nest. She gonna have babies any day now, an' she more into makin' sure she gots a safe place for birthin' than what on the menu."

Dante glanced at the snake cage on the other table. "Kinda cold, ain't it? I mean, 'bout what just gonna happen to her kids."

Wyatt shrugged. "They only rats, man." He looked at the snake cage, too. "They don't know nuthin' 'bout the future." He turned back to Dante. "*They* don't got big enough brains to let 'em make choices." Then he shrugged again. "Yo. If Havoc here got hungry enough, he eat his own kids."

"But wouldn't their mom try an' stop him?"

"Sure. But she ain't strong enough."

Wyatt put Havoc back in the cage, then filled a saucer with more food and set it next to the well-gnawed nesting box in the cage's far corner. "Chaos come out an' eat when she done with her nest."

Dante rubbed his crotch, wishing his body would forget what had happened: It hadn't even seemed like real sex. Fact was, the *memory* of holding Jasmine in his arms now seemed more satisfying than the actual act. Maybe Pook could explain it?

"So, y'all comin' upstairs with us, Wyatt? We got a couple more forties from Kelly on credit."

The fat boy smirked. "Y'all sellin' your soul for a buzz?" Then he saw Dante's scowl. "Okay. Long's you ain't gonna try an' cap me again."

"I said I was sorry, damnit!"

Wyatt tugged his boxers a little higher on his butt. "Well, I gotta say it kinda cool, you axin' Jinx over."

"Aw, he okay, I guess. Once you get down where he at. Look like you was right."

"Mmm. I right 'bout a lotta stuff, man. Too bad you don't listen more."

"Chill, Wyatt. Okay?"

Wyatt sighed. "Yeah. So, how Jinx doin' anyways?"

Dante smiled. "Better since he buzzed. He even talkin' when we come home, 'stead of always waitin' for somebody else to say somethin' first. He kinda like Radgi that way. Somethin' different 'bout him. It sorta make you wonder what he was like 'fore he start doin' crack."

"Yeah? So, how 'Willy'?"

"Huh? . . . Oh. Radgi a lot better'n he was this mornin' too. An', yo, man, he never touch nuthin' in the place all day."

"Mmm. Nuthin' you know 'bout yet, anyways. Maybe he just fly at coverin' his tracks."

"Naw. I put one my hairs on the kitchen drawer where the money is. Read 'bout that trick in a James Bond book. Radgi never touch nuthin', man. 'Cept cookin' himself some SpaghettiOs for lunch. An', he even wash up the pan."

"Maybe he read the same book?"

"Oh, shut up."

"So, what you gonna do 'bout him, Dante? What I sayin' is, it Thursday night now an' your dad be back Sunday. What he gonna think 'bout you cribbin' some sick homeless kid?"

"What you mean? Yo! We be Rasta! Rasta care 'bout people!"

Wyatt shook his head. "Wemarkabo."

From the living room came Mrs. Brown's bellow: "CHEO! IT TIME FOR YOUR BATH, HONEY!"

"HE CAN'T HEAR YOU!" roared Wyatt.

"HEAR, WHAT?" yelled Cheo.

"IT TIME . . ." Wyatt stepped to the bed and yanked the head-phones off Cheo's ears—". . . for your bath, dear little ass-wipe."

"Oh."

Cheo turned off the Walkman and rolled from the bed. Hitching his shorts halfway up, he padded out of the room. A few minutes later came the gurgle and splash of water. Dante got up. "Um, think you could snag us some beer, man? Them deuce dogs ain't goin' far for all us."

"Well, I guess. But, hell, Dante, this the second night runnin' you been buzzed."

"Yo, An' this the second night runnin' you come like my conscience, man. I *know* there school tomorrow. Stop worryin' 'bout me. I just finally startin' to chill with the flava for once in my life."

Wyatt scanned Dante's face, then sighed. "Okay. I get the café keys an' hook with you at the stairs."

"Cool. An' thanks, Wyatt. I'ma go piss. See ya in a minute."

Dante went into the bathroom. Cheo was already in the tub amid a froth of fluffy white bubbles. He was so fat he could float on his back. Dante stepped to the toilet, then pointed to a toy ship sitting high and dry on Cheo's big belly.

"Look like your tanker aground, man."

Cheo giggled. "It leak. Gonna have me a eco-disaster."

"*She*, man. Boats is always 'she.'" Dante buttoned his jeans, then leaned over and picked up the ship. "Her hull cracked. Here at the bow." He smiled. "What happen, she run up on them two big rocks? Didn't her captain see your lighthouse?"

Cheo giggled again. "Naw. I drop *her* on the floor."

Dante went to the medicine cabinet and found a box of Band-Aids. He stuck one over the crack in the ship's plastic hull. "Here, man. This oughta hold till she can find a safe port."

Cheo sat up and sailed the ship around a brown kneecap island. "Yo, Dante. Wanna take off your clothes an' play boats with me?"

Dante smiled again. "Well, I don't got time right now."

Cheo sighed. "Wyatt never do neither no more. He used to play boats with me all the time, till he got old."

"Maybe he just got too fat? Both you in that tub, there hardly be room for no water."

"Naw. You don't never get too fat to play, just too old." Cheo looked wise and tapped his forehead with a finger. "Up *here*. Pook still play with me sometimes."

"In the *tub?*"

"Sure. He know how to play real good." Cheo saw Dante's amazed expression and giggled again. "Yo, fool! He only like *ole* boys, the way you an' Wyatt scheme ole girls. With me, he be just like a kid. So, how come you can't be more like him?"

". . . Well, I wasn't born that way."

"So? Can't you learn?"

Dante smiled once more, picturing buff-bodied Pook playing boats in the bathtub. How could you think you ever knew what anybody was all about when your own homeys could still surprise you? "Well, I got friends waitin', Cheo. But tell you what, I'ma bring you down my ole tugboat tomorrow."

"An' play?"

"Been a long time since I sail *Bantu.*"

Dante left, going down the hall and crossing the living room, saying good night to Wyatt's mom, who sat on the sofa scowling at some TV show about black kids gaining self-esteem in state-sponsored concentration camps. He waited at the foot of the staircase until Wyatt came in with a sixer of Rolling Rock.

"Um, Wyatt? You ever seen Pook playin' with Cheo in the tub?"

The fat boy looked surprised. "Hell, I got pictures. So, where you been for the last thirteen years, fool? He played with you too, didn't he?"

It was funny, but Dante felt cheated somehow. "Yeah. But, not for a long time."

Upstairs, Dante paused after Pook opened the apartment door. It seemed another surprise to find his home full of homeys. The TV was tuned to *Rocko's Modern Life,* and the gas fire's flames flickered in the corner. Pook returned to the couch and sat down between Jinx and Radgi. Jinx sprawled with his shoes and socks off and his none-too-clean feet on the coffee tabletop. Only Radgi wore a shirt, and his greasy X cap as always. The forties Dante had scored from Kelly sat on the table; one empty, the other half-gone. Pook had made a huge bowl of microwave popcorn.

Wyatt pushed past Dante and entered. "Look like some kinda gang clubhouse," he murmured. "Shoulda brought my camera."

Dante shrugged and closed the door. "Look more like just bruthas to me."

"Pigs bust in, they call us a 'gang,' best believe that!" Wyatt grinned. "Complete with *two* crack addicts. Be on the sixer news tomorrow." Wyatt gave Dante a glance. "'Specially, they find what you stashed up here, man."

Dante made a face. "Oh, yeah. An' we call ourselves the Babylon Boyz."

Wyatt looked thoughtful. "Mmm, that kinda phat. Make a way cool tag. I can almost see it on a boxcar."

Dante felt Radgi's gaze as he crossed the room and sat down in his dad's big leather chair. The kid gave him a smile that seemed happy. But what did Dante care. After all, he'd just had real sex today . . . sort of. Dante snagged the half-empty O.E. and took a big hit, then turned his eyes to the TV screen. Rocko the wallaby was trying to cope with Babylonian bullshit. Dante kicked off his shoes and socks, pulled off his shirt, and settled to watch, but his mind kept drifting to Radgi. The kid couldn't crib here forever, but maybe until he got well.

Jinx was drunk, and Dante almost felt guilty about that, but it was a comfortable kind of careless kid-drunk where you kicked on a couch and felt safe and at peace with your homeys. His slack stomach slopped like a puddle of pudding when he swallowed, and he tilted the bottle up in both hands as if not strong enough to hold it in one. It might have been helping him more than a whole year in rehab.

Wyatt had plopped his bulk on the couch between Pook and Radgi and was now sipping malt and watching TV. Only Radgi seemed a little alone and apart from the other boys.

The phone rang in the kitchen. Dante got up to go answer,

and only Radgi seemed aware he was leaving the room. Coming into the kitchen, Dante glanced at the trash can in the corner; the garbage bag was still creased on the rim in the secret way he'd left it that morning. He lifted the phone off its hook on the wall, hoping it might be his dad calling, even if only to say he'd be gone one more day. But it was Kelly.

"Yo, kid, I think I got us a buyer. Can you bring the piece to school tomorrow?"

Again, Dante glanced at the trash can. It seemed funny, but now he wasn't sure he wanted to sell Air Touch's gun. It would kick to have green, but money was strange in a way; it only seemed important when you needed it. He needed thousands for his operation; not the few hundred the gun would bring. Even split between Wyatt and Pook, his share would be enough to cruise summer vacation but would get him no nearer to having his heart fixed. And, maybe he'd *need* that piece . . . especially if he was going to try to set up a major drug deal.

"Um . . . so, how much, Kelly?"

"Yo! Shush, fool! No names on the *phone!*"

". . . Oh. Yeah. Sorry, man."

"What it is, kid. If the steel all you say, I can get you four Franklins."

" . . . Well . . ."

"Yo, kid. I *earn* my commissions."

"Naw, it ain't that."

Kelly laughed. "Ooooo. Y'all thinkin' 'bout keepin' it, huh? Lotta G's do; 'specially this close to summer vacation. Y'all start trippin' on what most like to get you through alive . . . the gat or the green."

". . . Well, I can always borrow Wyatt's if I need one."

"Yo, kid. We do it like this. You bring it tomorrow, y'all gots you a sale. You don't, no prob. Okay? Just wanna say it ain't been easy settin' this up. Ain't many regulators round here like that one. Inquirin' minds wanna know. Hear what I sayin'?"

"Yeah. An', thanks, Kel . . . kid."

Kelly snickered. "Yo, y'all got somethin' goin' on?"

"Huh?"

"Just never figured you the type, kid."

Dante scowled at the phone. "Yeah? Well, maybe I just sick of bein' disenfranchised all the time."

Kelly laughed. "Yeah. Don't ya just hate that? See ya, kid. Peace."

Dante hung up. There were footsteps in the hallway, and he turned to see Pook helping Jinx to the bathroom. For a second he wondered if Jinx was going to puke, but the boy looked too happy for that. He was just too drunk to walk by himself, an arm slung loose over Pook's wide shoulders, stumbling along with his jeans half off and a big goofy grin on his face. Dante smiled and went back into the living room. *Ren and Stimpy* was on TV now. Stimpy had fallen in love with a fart.

"This kinda stuff what Congress say gonna replace PBS for kids' programmin'!" muttered Wyatt, taking a gulp of malt.

"Well," said Dante. "It a animal show, ain't it?"

Radgi giggled, turning amused eyes to Dante.

"So, you feelin' better, man?" Dante asked.

"Shhh!" said Wyatt. "This the *good* part; when Stimpy leave home to go look for his fart. Way educational. Who need to know 'bout lions in Kenya when you got quality programmin' like this."

"Um?" asked Radgi. "Isn't there a special nature channel?"

"It cost," said Dante. He smirked at Wyatt. "So, who need real lions when you got *The Lion King*?"

Wyatt made a face. Dante snagged the bottle and took a hit, then passed it to Radgi, who tilted it up with both hands like Jinx had done but seemed only to sip before handing it back. Dante took another swig and gave it to Wyatt. Now that he was here, he couldn't think of anything to say. Would Radgi be impressed that he'd had real sex? He didn't have to know *all* the details. But somehow the timing didn't seem right for such an important announcement. Dante was almost grateful when he had to go to the bathroom.

His bare feet were silent on the hallway floorboards. The bathroom door was open and light fanned out brightly. Not sure why, Dante hesitated and peeked in around the doorframe. Then he froze. His throat went tight and he could feel his heart pound in his chest.

Jinx and Pook stood by the bathtub. For the first instant Dante thought that Jinx was just too drunk to stand and Pook was holding him up. But it was way more than that! Jinx was naked, his jeans in a heap at his feet, and the soot-colored slop of his body enfolded in Pook's bronze, muscled arms.

Desperately, Dante's mind made excuses. It *couldn't* be what it looked like! Of *course* Jinx's jeans had slipped off; they hardly stayed on anyway. Jinx was drunk; maybe he'd busted into tears the way drunk kids sometimes did for no reason and Pook being Pook was just comforting him? But it wasn't like that at all. Pook was naked too. Dante just stood, staring, wanting to leave but somehow unable. He wondered why he was feeling like this. He'd known what Pook was for years, but he'd never actually seen him holding and kissing a boy before. In fact, he didn't think Pook ever had.

Dante's mind ran around in his skull like something trapped and refusing to accept it. In a way it was like finally seeing somebody get capped even though you'd been talking about it since you were toothless. His fists clenched. His nose got crinkly, and he felt sudden tears burn his eyes. Then came stupid, unreasoning rage . . . stupid because it was too much like jealousy cut with disgust. *Why Jinx?* Dante couldn't remember why he'd ever thought he cared enough for that miserable mess of a kid to go through the hell he'd gone through today. Pook could have done *better!* Jinx smelled like a dog, had hair like a rat's nest, and if his brains had been dynamite, he couldn't have blown his own nose!

Dante couldn't have stood there more than five seconds. His rage leaked away, leaving him strangely cold. All he could think now was that he hadn't even had a chance to tell Pook what had happened to *him* today. He slunk back down the hall, into the warm golden glow of the living room. He wasn't sick, he wasn't disgusted, he was just mad as hell and he didn't know why. The only relief was to find that *Ren and Stimpy* was over and Wyatt was on his feet to go home.

Dante came out to the head of the stairs with him. For a moment he thought of telling Wyatt what he'd just seen, but was afraid the fat boy would just make one of his usual jokes . . . like the whole thing was funny or something. Dante muttered a short, see-ya-later, and waited for the slow squeak of Wyatt's footsteps to fade down the dark spiral staircase. Then, still needing to piss, he went on the rickety little landing in back that passed for a fire escape and sent his stream arching into the night to spatter and rattle the lids of the trash cans below. He stood there a time, feeling the chilly Bay breeze on his body and hearing the city sounds and the occasional hoot of a tugboat or ship. He wished he had a cigarette . . . "chemically-dependent comfort." Finally, he went back inside.

Radgi was still on the couch, and gave Dante a curious look as if sensing that something had happened. Shadows came down the hall. Dante took his place in his father's big chair and waited. He wanted to see their faces, but gave them only an eye-corner glance because Pook would have read his own in an instant and he didn't want Pook to know he knew, yet. Maybe he wanted Pook to feel guilty? Or at least go through the motions?

They came in together, Jinx still too buzzed to walk by himself, but not so drunk that he couldn't have known what he'd done. Carefully, Dante studied his face: Jinx just looked peaceful. His jeans were back on, barely, and Pook's own were only half-buttoned. The smell that Dante expected was faint in the air. Radgi looked uneasy, scenting it too, but Dante ignored the kid and turned to face Pook. There was no guilt in Pook's eyes, and Dante wondered why he'd expected any. He hadn't planned words, but they came easily enough: "You can have my crib, man. I sleep out here tonight."

Jinx didn't seem to understand, or maybe he hadn't heard, but Pook met Dante's eyes a long moment and Dante realized it *had* been his first time. Strangely, Dante wondered if it had been "good."

Pook only nodded and then, helping Jinx, turned to go back up the hall. He looked like a young warrior guarding a precious thing. Dante almost called after him, the words on his lips, *least it didn't cost you ten dollars.*

But he didn't say them.

Radgi's eyes seemed to question as if suspecting whatever had happened had changed things for him too. He looked at his coat on the floor.

Dante picked up a bottle and forced down several huge swallows, then made himself shrug. "It Pook an' Jinx . . . They was . . . together. Maybe that what was wrong with Jinx all the time."

". . . Oh."

"I gonna sleep out here tonight. In this chair."

Surprisingly, Radgi smiled. "You're way cool, Dante."

Dante considered that. He didn't feel cool; only betrayed, even though that was stupid. A news show had started: an interview with some old white suit who'd once had something to do with education. He was saying that inner-city kids would be a lot better off if all government subsidies were cut, including food stamps and housing and aid to unwed mothers. He went on to say that he wouldn't send his own children to any school that gave away condoms, then added that gay rights was one of the reasons the American divorce rate was so high, and finished with an opinion that funding should be stopped to find a cure for AIDS because only those dregs of society who didn't believe in traditional American values got it.

Dante snagged the remote and killed the TV, then picked up the bottle again. "'Traditional American values' used to mean keepin' us slaves like we was animals. Later on they meant we had to ride in back of buses. Don't seem like much changed. Y'all wanna get drunk with me, Radgi?"

"Isn't that bad for your heart?"

Dante regarded the bottle and forced a laugh he didn't feel. "So is bein' a fool."

Radgi only looked serious. "So, why are you buggin' over Pook? I thought he was your homey? An', I thought you liked Jinx too? Both of 'em look happy."

Dante felt like crying again. "Yeah. All of a sudden everybody happy but me! It like somethin' change. Like somethin' *dirty* come into this house." He put down the bottle. "But, it ain't you, man. Don't go thinkin' that. Um, you sure you don't wanna get drunk?"

Radgi smiled faintly. "Go to sleep, Dante. You got school tomorrow."

"Aw, hell, maybe you right." Dante sighed and slumped back, spreading his feet on the tabletop. "Least I don't gotta go to rehab no more."

He closed his eyes. Sleep came quickly and he didn't see Radgi get up and pad quietly to the hall closet to bring back a blanket. Radgi tucked it around Dante before turning out the light and laying down on the couch.

A long time later in the deep of the night, Dante got up. There was something he had to do, even if he wasn't sure what it was. He stood for what seemed like hours looking down at Radgi's sleeping form; the kid's face peaceful in the flickering glow from the fire. Dante found himself smiling because Radgi still wore his cap. Then his smile faded and he walked up the hall. Pook would tell him what he had to do.

Dante stopped in the bedroom doorway. A square of blue-tinted light from the street lamp spread over the blankets of his bed. For a moment he wondered if he was seeing himself asleep in Pook's muscled arms. In thirteen years they'd never slept together like that . . . but then he remembered. The toy tugboat sat on his desk. Quietly, Dante came in and picked it up, then took it into the bathroom.

The faint scent of Radgi and bubbles still seemed to linger in the air. It reminded him of what he had to do. Putting the bathtub stopper in place, he turned on the water . . . low, because he didn't want to wake anyone. He set the toy boat in the slowly filling tub, then slipped off his jeans and shorts. Now for the bubbles.

Cheo was in the tub when Dante returned. It seemed no surprise to find him there, all round and roly-poly. For some reason he was wearing Radgi's cap. He grinned up at Dante. "Wanna come in an' play with me?"

Dante looked down at the boy: His skin seemed the same brilliant brown as Radgi's. Dante smiled. "Here come the bubbles. Now everythin' be all clean again."

"Dante?"

"Huh?" Dante blinked. Then his whole body jerked as if jabbed with a prod. Images flashed and spun through his mind like a videotape snapping. He felt his heart skip and falter like an attack was coming, but it was only the shock of waking on his feet in the bathroom without a clue how he'd come there or what he was doing.

Radgi stood in the doorway, hand on the light switch, barefoot but otherwise dressed as always in jeans, grimy T-shirt, and cap. His face looked sleepy; eyes only half-wide in wonder. "I had to go to the bathroom. An' then I heard the water running an' you talkin' . . . um, the door was open."

Radgi's eyes went to the tub. Dante looked too, jolted again when he saw his tugboat bobbing on an empty steaming sea. Then, he stared in horror at what he'd been about to pour in. Torn open in his hand was one of the plastic cocaine packages!

A whimper welled up in his throat. All strength seemed to drain from his body. Still clutching the package, he sank to his knees, his chest against the bathtub rim. Tears flooded his eyes, dropping silently into the water. "Oh, shit!" he moaned. "Oh, *shit!*"

"Dante!" Radgi ran to his side, kneeling awkwardly and grabbing Dante's shoulders. "What is it, Dante? Are you having an attack? What should I do?"

The tears wouldn't stop, and Dante didn't care. He let the package fall between his legs and covered his face with his hands. Radgi's arms went around him, pulling him close.

"Dante! What's wrong? I'll get Pook!"

Radgi's words seemed to filter through fog. It was like coming out of an attack . . . confusion and fear and the terrible feeling of being alone.

"No!" Dante choked back sobs. "No, man. I okay." He started to raise his head, but then let it fall against Radgi's shoulder. "I wish I was dead!"

Radgi's grip tightened. Small fingers gently brushed back the dreds from Dante's face. "No, you don't! Dante, what's *wrong?* Tell me what happened!"

Slowly, Dante lifted his head once more, eyes wide and staring at the familiar room as if seeing it for the first time. His voice broke in amazement. "I musta been walkin' in my sleep!"

One arm still around Dante, Radgi took his hand and held it. "But, that happens."

Dante turned to look into Radgi's eyes. "It does?"

Radgi studied him, then smiled a careful smile. "Sure. Almost everybody does it sometimes. That's what my mom told me when I was little." Radgi's smile widened slightly. "I used to do it a lot." Then Radgi's eyes softened. "Mom used to tell me our people believe it's God takin' you for a walk in the moonlight. To show you somethin' special that nobody else can see. He always holds your hand. That's why nobody who walks in their sleep ever falls."

"But, *I* never done it before!"

"Most of the time you don't even know. Unless somebody wakes you up. Like me."

". . . Oh. Yeah, I seen this movie. But, you ain't s'posed to wake up sleepwalkers."

"I didn't do it on purpose."

Dante looked around once more. "I 'member we had us a talk 'bout that stuff in health, science an' sex-ed class last year. But, teacher never said nuthin' 'bout takin' no walks with Jah. All she say be that sleepwalkin' can mean you . . . *disturbed.*"

Radgi didn't seem sure whether to smile or not. "Well,

when you're out on the street at night you see a lot of 'disturbed' people walkin' around, but none of them are sleepin'."

Now it was Dante who smiled. "Don't s'pose none of 'em look like they walkin' with Jah, neither."

"Well, it was probably just a little-kid story anyhow." Radgi pointed to the tub. "Maybe you just wanted to take a bath? Being a little dirty is nothing to get disturbed about."

Radgi's scent was in Dante's nostrils. It seemed a comfort to have the kid's sleepy-warm body so close to his own. Dante wiped his face, then quickly shoved the package out of sight under the tub. He wasn't sure if it was shame he felt that Radgi had found him like this, but there was relief at having someone to talk to.

"It was like a dream! At first I thought I was gonna take a bath with Wyatt's little brother, Cheo." Dante gave Radgi an uncertain glance. "I mean, I was gonna play boats with him. He only eight, an' he still down with that sorta kid-stuff, y'know." Dante swallowed, wondering how Radgi would react to such a picture.

But Radgi only smiled once more, gazing down where the toy tug rocked on the ripples from the trickling faucet. "Is that your boat?"

"Huh? Oh. Yeah. Hell, I had that forever, man. My dad give her to me when I was way little." Dante felt his face growing warm, and added, "I'ma give it to Cheo tomorrow."

Radgi gave the boat a gentle push, sailing it across the tub. "Why?"

"Well, I guess I just be too ole for playin' toy boats no more." Dante sailed it back to Radgi.

Radgi looked wistful. "I kinda wish we could play boats. You an' me."

Uncertain, Dante looked at Radgi again. Then he turned back to the tub and nudged the boat with his fingertip. "Go back to sleep, brutha. I see you in the mornin'."

Radgi seemed to want to say something else, but then got up awkwardly and walked to the door. Dante stared down at the little boat. He wished he could call Radgi back.

And do what? Play boats?

Radgi paused in the doorway. "This is the first place I ever felt safe, Dante. Here with you an' your homeys." Another small smile crossed the kid's face. "With the Babylon Boyz. I heard what Wyatt said." Radgi sighed and gazed at the toy boat. "It's just so hard to trust anybody."

Dante nodded. "Yeah. An', you right 'bout what you say that day after school: It hard to make friends when you don't got not choices." He smiled. "G'night, brutha. An' thanks for cluein' me 'bout that moonlight walkin' with Jah." He watched Radgi leave, then looked down at the floor. The torn-open package had spilled about a teaspoon of powder onto the tile. He wondered how much money a few blows like that would bring. Paper money, powder money, why should he feel any different about what they could buy in Babylon?

He carefully picked up the package so it wouldn't spill anymore, then stood for a time at the toilet. Had he really been walking with Jah, and had He showed him the way to make his life clean again?

Or, just how to be a nice clean little victim?

Finally, he got a roll of medical tape from the cabinet and carefully patched the plastic.

"Dante?"

A hand touched his shoulder and Dante opened his eyes. He was in his dad's chair with a blanket around him. He blinked, momentarily confused by the jumbled memory mix of the last night. Had it all been a dream and now he would find nothing changed? Jinx was standing close. His stomach overlapped the arm of the chair and his breasts hung loose as he leaned forward. Dante's nose wrinkled at his unwashed smell and the scent of male sex. Jinx and Pook together had been no dream. His eyes flicked to find Radgi still wrapped in blankets and asleep on the couch.

"Uh," said Jinx, "can I borrow a pair of your socks, Dante? Pook say to axe."

Dante's eyes came back to Jinx. Part of him wanted to kick the kid's sorry ass down the stairs. Instead, he blew air and nodded. "Yeah. Sure. Why the hell not."

The boy's face brightened. "Thanks, Dante." He turned toward the hallway.

Dante felt an urge to wipe his shoulder where Jinx had touched him, but glanced at the clock instead. "Yo, Jinx. Why don't you take a bath? There lots of time."

"Zuh?" Jinx paused as if to consider a new concept, then nodded obediently. "Okay."

Dante sprawled back in the chair, watching Jinx shuffle away in his dirty jeans, their ragged cuffs dragging the floor while his belly wobbled like a half-filled hot water bottle. He looked half-asleep as always, but somehow secure as if he were walking with Jah in the moonlight. Dante sighed. Why shouldn't Jinx feel safe? Now he had Pook, and if Jah was a boy, He'd probably *be* Pook.

"Um, Jinx?"

The boy stopped and turned around. "Zuh?"

"Try on a pair of my jeans. They in the third dresser drawer. They might sorta fit if you don't button 'em. You can put yours in the dirty clothes box up the hall."

Jinx looked amazed. "Zuh?"

Dante scowled. "An' stop sayin' 'zuh,' damnit! Make you sound like a retard!"

"Uh . . . okay, Dante. An', thanks."

"Yeah." Dante glanced again at Radgi's peaceful form, then got up and went to the kitchen.

The bag was once more turned down over the garbage can's rim . . . so he had put the package back with the others. Air Touch's gun was still in there too. He heard the bathwater running, and was relieved to remember he'd drained the tub and taken the tugboat out. He loaded the Mr. Coffee, then headed for his room. Pook was just getting out of bed. He was naked and beautiful, and to cover his body with clothes seemed as much of a sin as putting pajamas on a panther. Dante only nodded to him while going to the dresser and yanking open his underwear drawer. He kept his back turned while changing his shorts, but could see Pook's puzzled expression in the closet door mirror. Pook spread his hands.

"Why you pissed at me, Dante?"

"Who say I am?"

"Dante? What I s'posed to say?"

Dante jerked open another drawer and grabbed a fresh pair of socks. "Ain't nuthin' you s'posed to say. Ain't like you went an' jack my bed out from under me. I told you to take it, remember."

"But why you pissed, Dante?"

Dante turned to face Pook. "I had sex. Yesterday. With a *girl.* Guess that make us one-an'-one, huh."

Pook cocked his head. "Why you never tell me?"

Dante shrugged again. "Guess I never got time. 'Sides, it wasn't 'good for me.' Wasn't nuthin' like love at all. So, was it 'good' for you last night? Was it everythin' you always hoped it would be with the *boy* of your dreams?"

Pook looked surprised and hurt, and a part of Dante enjoyed that, while another part was somehow ashamed of enjoying it. He added, "Jinx takin' a bath. Prob'ly the first one he ever had. Y'all hurry, you can jump in an' shampoo his hair or somethin'. Jah know he need it!"

Pook rose from the bed and came over. He reached to take Dante's shoulders, but Dante stepped back, those same scents of Jinx and boy-sex filling his nostrils, mingled with Pook's own male smell. Pook let his hands fall to his sides.

"Dante? It just *happen.*"

Dante yanked up his jeans and scowled. "Uh-huh. You sayin' you never even thought about Jinx before?" His eyes narrowed further in sudden suspicion. "Maybe that why y'all so up for me 'helpin'' him, huh? Yo, you wanted to help that sorry-ass sucka, *you* shoulda gone to rehab with him! *You* shoulda wasted your god-damn first time fuckin' on a dirty floor like a couple of stupid rats!"

Pook frowned. "Yo, Dante. You figure we all know each other or somethin'? Like, there some secret sign for showin' each other who we are?"

Dante snorted. "Hell! You figure you somethin' special, man? A new species, maybe? Shit! Queers ain't the only kids who don't know who they are!" Dante pushed past Pook and stalked out. Jinx stood naked in the bathroom doorway, the Mr. Bubble bottle in one hand.

"Um, Dante? Okay I use this?"

Dante wanted to walk past in disgust. Jinx's body was living proof that some people should keep their shapes secret. But Dante just shrugged. "Sure." Then he added, "We all goin' down to breakfast in few minutes. Guess you might as well come too."

A little while later all the boys were at a table in Wyatt's café. Radgi seemed to be better this morning and sat beside Dante nibbling at sausage and eggs. Normally, Pook would have been on one side of Dante and Wyatt on the other, but now Pook and Jinx sat together across the table. Wyatt did most of the talking, scheming the tag-team hit for tomorrow. Radgi did most of the listening. Jinx added a careful word now and then, seeming excited to be a part of something for once in his life, and never once said, "Zuh." He gave Dante occasional glances that dripped gratitude and disgusted Dante all the more because he somehow felt like a pimp for bringing Jinx home. Could you pimp love? Dante didn't know. He managed to have his eyes somewhere else whenever Pook looked at him.

The café was crowded as usual with breakfasting truckers and dock workers. Conversation and crockery clatter filled the steamy air. Dante got up once to play "Kingston Town" on the jukebox, and Radgi listened and smiled at the words of the song. Dante's backpack lay under his chair with Air Touch's big gun inside. He wasn't sure how he was going to get it past the metal detector at school. Wyatt could smuggle it through, but he hadn't asked yet. He was just about to catch Wyatt's eye when he saw Kelly walk in from the street. Wyatt noticed the Korean boy too and gave Dante a smirk.

"Look like The Collector come for his forty-dog money. Nowhere to run when people know where you live."

Dante didn't want to deal with Kelly in front of everyone. He got up and snagged his backpack, then headed Kelly off and led him out around the corner in the bright morning sunlight.

"Sorry to bother y'all at breakfast," said Kelly as they walked to the alley behind the café. "But I got a long buyer. Deal goin' down at eight-thirty. If you ain't changed your mind. I have four bills for you tomorrow."

Despite last night's uncertainty, Dante now just wanted to get rid of the gun so at least one dirty thing would be out of his life. "Okay." He pulled it from his pack, gleaming in the sun, and waited while Kelly gave it an expert scoping.

"Everything you say it was, kid. See ya in history." Kelly slipped the big pistol into his own pack, then pulled out a can of Krylon. "Here's the red Wyatt wanted." He grinned. "Things happen fast when people smell green."

"Yeah," said Dante. "Like flies on shit." He shrugged. "Just take what me an' Wyatt owe you out what I got comin'. Okay?"

Kelly laughed and slapped Dante's shoulder. "You cool, kid. True to the game an' down with your homeys." He dug in his pocket. "Here's a extra nozzle. They like friends, can't have too many. So, where y'all hittin'?"

"Wyatt got a new tag he want to try on a boxcar." Dante had another thought. "Maybe if it come phat, we hit that big park up on Broadway."

Kelly whistled. "You kids gettin' blatant! That bringin' it home to Babylon for sure! They shoot taggers on sight up there!"

Dante returned to the restaurant and handed Radgi the apartment keys. "Here, man. You can chill in the crib today." Then he added, "Um, maybe you like to do somethin' later on?"

Radgi searched Dante's eyes, then smiled. "That would be cool."

Radgi turned to Dante with a look of wonder. "I didn't know you could play boats for real."

Dante smiled. "Well, ain't much of a boat."

The afternoon sun was warm and bright, and Radgi's brilliant brown skin seemed to glow. Without the baggy jacket, his big belly ballooned his grimy T-shirt to give him a clumsy cartoonish shape that somehow invited a hug. He bent awkwardly forward, hands on knees for balance, peering over the edge of the ramshackle wharf at an old wooden skiff that nuzzled a weed-grown piling below. The boat was ten feet long, paintless and scarred, splattered by seagulls and moored by a red-rusted chain.

"Is it *yours?*"

Dante smiled again: Radgi was gazing at the battered little boat as if it were a sleek sailing yacht. "*She,* man. Boats is always 'she.' She belong to my dad. They use her for paintin' an' workin' on the tug."

Radgi moved to the top of the rickety wooden ladder. "Can we get in her, Dante?"

Dante grinned and pulled a tarnished brass key from his jeans pocket. "We can do more'n that, man. We can go for a cruise if you want."

"You can sail her?"

"I can row her. Climb on down an' get aboard. Watch that third rung, it loose."

Radgi hesitated a moment, but then got carefully onto the ladder. Dante watched, concerned because the boy's bulging belly made the descent anything but easy, and was relieved when Radgi managed to reach the boat and clamber clumsily back to the stern seat. Dante climbed down, got in the bow, unlocked the padlock, coiled the chain, and pushed the boat away from the wharf. Moving to the middle seat, he slipped the oars into the locks. Then, with a few expert strokes he swung the boat around and rowed out of the wharf shadow into the sparkling sunlight. The boat was waterlogged and heavy and bearded with seaweed, but Dante pulled stroke with the slow, easy rhythm of experience. He wore a tank top, a tight old white one of Pook's, and felt proud that Radgi seemed to notice how rowing defined his small biceps and chest.

"So, where you wanna go, man?"

Radgi was staring around. "Everything looks so different from here on the water! The city almost looks pretty!"

Dante grinned. "Yeah. I know what you sayin'. Boats are cool that way. They give you another . . . um . . ."

"Perspective?"

"Yeah. That what it is. Maybe you need perspectives to make better choices?" Dante stopped rowing and held the oar handles together in one hand while pointing with the other. "That be Treasure Island over there. An' that one be Alcatraz. Way past it you can see the Golden Gate Bridge."

Radgi turned to gaze where Dante pointed. The kid's face suddenly seemed to hold a strange yearning. "That's the Pacific Ocean, huh? Boats go across it."

Dante nodded and began rowing once more; nowhere in particular, just parallel to the shoreline. "Ships do. But they big." He glanced down at himself and sighed. "I ain't even strong enough to row us to the Bay Bridge. Too many currents an' tide rips." He thought a moment, then added, "Pook prob'ly could. But we can cruise around here for a while."

"What if we had a motor, Dante? Could we cross the ocean?"

Dante smiled. "Jah's sea is so great, an' my boat be so small. That a sorta prayer my dad taught me." He studied Radgi, noting that wistful expression again. "So, where would you wanna go?"

Radgi was quiet for a time, face turned toward the west, eyes strangely wistful in the shadow of the cap's crumpled visor. Seagulls circled and cried overhead and wavelets slapped softly against the boat's bow with liquid musical sounds. "How far is Australia, Dante?"

Dante tried to remember the world geography maps from school. "A long ways." He pulled a few more strokes, then rested the oars again, seeing Radgi still gazing toward the Golden Gate. Then, gently, and not certain why, he reached over and removed Radgi's cap. He wasn't sure what he'd expected, but Radgi's hair, bushy, woolly, and wild, shone like burnished copper in the golden sunlight and made him look more than ever like the Aboriginal boy in Pook's book. Radgi seemed only slightly surprised, turning to face Dante, eyes questioning. Red lips, rusty hair, skin so brilliant brown it glowed, the dusting of freckles over the wide, bridgeless nose, and those big bronze-green eyes. Again, Dante felt the urge to hug the boy. He suspected that Radgi could sense the attraction, and smiled guiltily as he handed the cap back. He tensed when his fingers brushed Radgi's.

"Who are you, man? Where you come from? You ain't like no other brutha I ever met before."

Radgi didn't speak for a moment, still holding the cap but searching Dante's eyes. Then he turned and pointed toward the East Bay hills, where big expensive houses smirked down on West Oakland. "I used to live up there, but . . ." He faced Dante, looking uncertain, but then seeming to make a decision. "My mom was from Australia."

Dante felt the tension fade. He sighed, echoing Radgi, and nodded. The current was carrying the boat toward a shore of slimy black mud and rust-rotted junk, where a few jagged pilings thrust up like fangs through a tideline of trash. He dipped the oars and began to row once more. "Well, that be one little mystery solved. Fact is, Wyatt already figure you from there. The desert be red in Australia, huh?"

Radgi nodded. "I've only seen pictures. My mom had a lot of pictures. She painted them. Some were like landscapes she remembered, and some were sort of spiritual things our people used to do with different-colored sand."

"Your people the ones who believe about walkin' with Jah in the moonlight?"

Radgi looked thoughtful and trailed a finger in the water. "My mom used to tell me a lot of old stories like that." Radgi shifted position to gaze out over the Bay. "She got discovered, I guess. By white people; way out there in the desert. They started buying her paintings for lots of money. She got famous. An' rich. She came here on a tour and I guess she just stayed." Radgi's face darkened a little. "Maybe she got sort of trapped. I don't think she liked this place very much. Even up there in those hills."

"Babylon," murmured Dante, still pulling slow strokes, sweat now sheening his ebony skin and sticking the tank top tight to his body. "My dad say healthy people can always sense when somethin' sick, an' wanna get away from it." He paused to point out a refinery wharf. "Back in the ole days they used to use canaries in cages to check out tanker ships to see if it was safe to go down inside after they was empty. Canaries be more sensitive to poison in the air than people. If the canary freaked, they knew it was bad. Sometimes the canary even died. . . . Maybe kids are like canaries in Babylon."

Radgi fingered his greasy black cap. "That's how I feel. It's like I'm trapped in some cage an' there's poison all around in the air. My mom felt that way too." Radgi put the cap back on, looking more like a rugged child again. "There was this man. He was white . . . that's how I happened. I don't know much about him except that he was supposed to be my mom's manager, but he treated her bad an' spent all her money. He got her into drugs . . . or maybe she got herself into 'em 'cause she was lonely an' didn't understand a lot of stuff about living here. She stopped painting. Maybe she just couldn't anymore. Then the man left with just about all the money. That was about a year ago. We kept on having to move into worse an' worse places."

Dante saw tears in Radgi's eyes. Radgi wiped them away and turned toward the Golden Gate. "My mom died of an overdose. Last year. I came home from school an' found her. There wasn't anybody to help me. The only thing I could think of to do was call 911. The cops came an' took me someplace. Maybe it was jail, 'cause they locked me in a room with bars. Nobody ever seemed sad about my mom or acted liked they cared. Finally some people came an' took me someplace else an' locked me in again. It's funny that the first thing they do to help is lock you up. For a while they said they were tying to find my mom's family in Australia, but then somebody else said I belong to this country. I finally got put in a high-risk minority youth readjustment home."

"A, *what?*" said Dante. "Oh, hell."

"I ran away. I wanted to be down here by the water. I thought I could sneak on a ship an' get to Australia an' find my own people. But it don't work like that."

Dante rested on the oars again, letting the boat drift. He wanted more than ever to hug Radgi; to give comfort. Pook could have done that natural as breathing, but Dante didn't know how to hug a boy he didn't know. Instead, he glanced toward a distant freighter that was heading out to sea. "It only worked back in the ole days. Ships are run different now. An', people gotta have pieces of paper to prove who they are an' where they belong." He looked again toward the Gate and the open ocean beyond. "I wish I could row out of Babylon. But I ain't strong enough."

Radgi smiled a little. "Being with you is almost as good as really getting away."

"Thanks." Dante took up the oars once more and turned the boat back toward the wharf. Radgi reached out and put a small brown hand over Dante's black one. There was warmth in the touch, but shyness came over Radgi's face.

"How do you feel about me, Dante?"

The question was unexpected. "Um . . . well, it hard to describe. It be sorta wantin' to know more about you . . . an' somethin' like *carin'* what happen to you." Dante took a breath. "In a way it like I want you to be . . . safe. An' happy. An', like I can't be them things myself till you are."

Radgi looked strangely sad. "Would it be good for you if I left?"

Dante groaned. "*Please* don't axe me that! Ain't nuthin' been 'good for me' since . . . well, I don't know when."

Radgi touched Dante's hand once more, carefully. "Thanks for playing boats with me."

Dante forced a smile, then began rowing again. "Anytime, homey." He pulled long strokes, giving himself to the rhythm while his mind drifted. *Why* did he care about Radgi? He rowed steadily, secretly studying Radgi, who, with big round tummy and soft chubby chest, hardly even looked like much of a boy. Even less of a boy than Jinx. Maybe what Pook saw in Jinx was somebody he wanted to be safe and happy with?

Then, from the corner of his eye he noticed a gleaming black shape on the shoreline. His heart faltered a moment when he recognized Air Touch's Viper! He saw the car stop at about the same place where he'd picked up the gun two nights ago. Air Touch got out and began searching among the container trailers and trash. Even at this distance Dante could see that his movements looked painful and stiff. Then Dante's eyes narrowed to slits: Let the stupid house-nigger search for his shit till Babylon sank in the sea! Kelly had done the gun deal and would have the money tomorrow. *So there, punk-ass fool!*

Radgi hadn't seen Air Touch yet, and Dante didn't want him to. He swung the boat's bow toward the Bay Bridge again, putting Radgi's back to the shore. He pulled hard on the oars, ignoring the warning pains in his chest, getting away from the shoreline before turning for the safety of the wharf. He was probably being paranoid: Air Touch couldn't have recognized them this far away, and he'd never suspect that two Babylon Boyz would be doing something as nice and clean as playing boats.

Dear Miss Kim . . .

Mr. Pak put down the pen and turned toward the door as the warning bell sounded. This would be trouble, and he'd sensed it when the thunder of a big American automobile engine had come rumbling up to the curb outside. The young men around the street lamp pole had gone quiet. Another bad sign. There was none of the usual crowding the car and whining and begging for money, though they could smell it. Even the boys who hovered at the doorway in hope of someone buying them beer stepped aside in silence as a young muscle-bulked black man in a snug leather coat swaggered past them.

Mr. Pak's eyes flicked to the clock: It was near enough time that he could have and should have been closed, but he'd been preoccupied with wording his letter and allowed himself to become careless. This was no life for a man to lead, chained to a counter and tensing like a rabbit whenever someone entered. He'd been shot three times in as many years, and robbed so often, he'd lost count long ago. Even in Korea he had never been so foolish to believe that life would be easy in America; yet he'd never imagined such a fearful existence in the world's richest nation.

He lay the letter aside. The young man was coming straight to the counter without so much as a glance at the malt in the cooler or the bottles of liquor and wine on the shelves . . . another bad sign. Yet for a moment, hope rose in Mr. Pak: The young man seemed so arrogant that he might be a plainclothes policeman come for free coffee kept fresh like an offering to insolent gods. The cops always took more than coffee, of course . . . took whatever they wanted in exchange for their unreliable presence. At least in Korea paying for protection had been a mutually honorable agreement, but here what passed for the law called it bribery, pretended to despise it, even threatened you for offering it, but took it smirking all the same like children who had never learned honor.

Children, yes! America seemed like a land of children: greedy, whining, spoiled children . . . and deadly children playing with guns. Some wore uniforms that granted them power to bully, extort, and kill, while others wore uniforms of a different kind, which entitled them to the same. There was no reasoning with spoiled children . . . they wanted, they took what they wanted, killed if they didn't get what they wanted, and sometimes killed even after they got it. Life in America was far from cheap, but death could often be bought for the price of a frown, a look, or the wrong tone of voice.

This was no cop, Mr. Pak realized; those overgrown boys on the sidewalk would never have cowed to the "law." Now they were moving away, not wanting to witness but slinking into the shadows like jackals in hope of scavenging scraps. This had happened before; Mr. Pak left for dead as the jackals grabbed all they could carry and smashed what they couldn't, while the alarm screamed for help that never came in time, if at all. A small sigh escaped him even as his body prepared for the shock of a possible bullet.

The black-coated figure came up to the counter: a handsome young man, but with bruises on his face and hate in his eyes. Mr. Pak's hand stayed under the counter, hovering between the alarm bell button and the cheap Chinese pistol his son had provided; a new replacement for those the smirking cops stole, to be used for what Kelly called "throw downs."

The young man's face was a study in well-practiced cruelty. His voice had a cop's tone of supreme arrogance. "Where's Kelly?"

Mr. Pak felt slight relief: Perhaps this was business? He knew of Kelly's enterprises, but the boy would have been doing similar things in Korea . . . though with more honorable motives. In America, too, bettering yourself seemed impossible within a strangling system of laws no one valued. Maybe with a wife, someone to share the burden, they could all someday escape this Babylon.

Mr. Pak relaxed a little. His hand moved from the gun to poise on the edge of the counter. He could see that the young man knew he had done this. Still, Mr. Pak was worried: This was not the sort Kelly dealt with. Maybe it would be best to say that his son wasn't home?

The young man saw his hesitation, and a scowl tightened lips that were swollen and cut. "Don't fuck with me, gook! I know he upstairs. Get his yellow ass down here. *Now!*"

Mr. Pak's eyes flicked to the front doorway . . . the deserted doorway. The jackals were all out of sight, but waiting. The pitiful plea in the window that read FREE COFFEE FOR LAW ENFORCEMENT OFFICERS would protect him no more than it ever had. And he knew now that this big hateful child was here for something more than what was in the cash register. Too late he realized he should have grabbed the gun; should have coldly emptied its magazine into this overgrown boy . . . just as coldly as this boy would kill him if he didn't get what he wanted.

Maybe he could still reach the gun? But, no; the boy's hand had gone to the pocket of his coat and there was no chance now. Mr. Pak's mouth went dry, but he kept his expression calm. "I will call him."

Carefully, Mr. Pak moved out from behind the counter. There was still a hope: He and his son had worked out a code. To call up the staircase, "Kelly, here is a friend," would bring him down, but to say, "Kelly, I need you," would have him instantly phoning the police. Yet it had taken almost twenty minutes for the law to come last time, and this evil child could kill and be gone in seconds. There was no choice after all. Mr. Pak parted the curtain and called up the dark stairwell, "Kelly! Here is a friend!"

The big boy nodded, his hand still in his pocket. "Get your ass back by the counter, an' don't even *think* about that gun." He seemed to consider, then his swollen lips formed a thin smile. "Chill out, *papa-san*. I just wanna axe your kid a few questions. He gimme the answers, everythin' flow." The smile changed to a smirk. "It business. Money business. You people got no trouble understandin' that."

Mr. Pak did as told, praying that this just might be "business" after all. He would speak to Kelly later about the company he kept! The big boy stepped casually to the cooler, took out a Magnum 40, and twisted off the cap. He drank deep. Mr. Pak's breath came easier now, though he still whispered prayers, hearing the door open above and the pad of his son's bare feet descending the steep wooden steps. Yes, he would speak long and hard to Kelly about this kind of "business"! Money meant survival, but life had to be more than survival to have any meaning.

Kelly parted the curtain and stepped into the room, blinking in the glare of the big naked bulbs after the shadowy stairwell. He wore only shorts, and Mr. Pak felt a surge of pride . . . a fine, healthy son who never would have grown to such size and handsomeness in Korea. But then he saw his son freeze in shock, eyes going wide, and the welcoming smile as if for Dante and Pook drop from his lips. His voice was toneless, flat, like a doctor's pronouncement of death: "Air Touch."

The terror on his son's face was too much to bear. Mr. Pak spun around and lunged across the counter in a desperate grab for the gun. Air Touch's hand whipped free of his coat, and two big-bore shots blasted the silence. Two more followed. Mr. Pak's body slammed the countertop, then twisted and jerked before sliding off and crashing to the floor. Kelly stood frozen, one hand clenched on the curtain so hard, a string of beads broke and scattered with a dry, rattling sound. Air Touch turned to face him, the big stainless-steel Smith & Wesson smoking in his hand.

"Recognize this, little gook?"

The booming bass rumble of a sixteen-cylinder E. M. D. engine was a sound almost more felt than heard. All the boys paused — Wyatt, Radgi, and Jinx — with spray cans in hand, and glanced up the tracks toward the slowly approaching locomotive. Radgi, about to fill in a big letter *Y* with a swirl of silver, gave Dante an uncertain look. "Um, what do we do now?"

Dante smiled. "Chill, man. Ain't them train people we worry about, it the yard pigs in their pickups."

Jinx and Wyatt had already gone back to work, adding the final touches to a big bright tag on the side of a rusty old boxcar. Done in red, green, and yellow with gloss black outlines and chrome silver accents was BABYLON BOYZ in phat hip-hop style. Jinx was just tailing the *Z*, while Wyatt was signing in black. All the kids were shirtless except Radgi; Pook in cutoffs with his backpack, the muscled pony boy who toted the paint and expedition supplies. Wyatt wore his Big Smiths, and Jinx an old pair of Dante's Boss jeans that he seemed proud of, even though they were way too tight and his stomach flopped over in front. Dante was in his best blue Ryes, while Radgi wore the same clothes as always: his old SilverTabs, grimy white tee, and greasy X cap turned backward. Finished painting, he smiled at Dante and pointed. "Jinx is pretty good at this, huh?"

Dante frowned. Jinx had stuck to Pook like a puppy all during school the day before, though he'd spent last night at his own crib. Dante had changed the sheets before bedding down with Pook. Maybe that had been a childish thing to do—Jinx's dirt was only the ordinary kind—but then so was coming cold to Pook, even though there seemed no logical reason for an attitude. Pook and Jinx seemed happy, and maybe he was just still in shock about the whole thing? It *couldn't* be jealousy, though it was funny that he felt as if Pook owed him an apology for *something*. Wyatt had found out; or maybe Pook had told him. It was typical that he accepted it all and welcomed Jinx to the posse with just a dumb joke or two. Dante hadn't told Wyatt about Jasmine in the rehab room, and now it didn't even seem worth mentioning.

He nodded. "Yeah. Jinx got a talent for taggin', all right. But, so do you, man." He stepped back and studied the work. "Cool the way our tag gonna be travelin' all over the country." He glanced back up the tracks. The locomotive was still rumbling slowly toward them. The engineer must have seen them by now, but he didn't blow the whistle. Dante touched Wyatt's shoulder. "Maybe we best bail, man. That guy might be callin' the yard pigs on his phone, an' you can't run very fast."

Wyatt nodded. "Gimme one more minute. Ain't nuthin' worth doin' if it ain't done right."

Radgi looked uneasy again. "I'm not very good at runnin' either."

Dante smiled: If anything, Radgi was even worse at it than Wyatt, but since everything the team did was timed to the fat boy's top speed, it had seemed safe to bring Radgi along. Dante had decided that when his dad got home tomorrow, they'd somehow get the kid to the hospital for a checkup. Kelly was supposed to come over tonight with the money from Air Touch's gun, so maybe they'd be able to afford whatever medical help Radgi needed. Dante frowned again . . . even if he wasn't able to sell the cocaine he now carried.

Wyatt and Jinx began loading the spray cans into Pook's pack. Dante tugged at his own pack straps. He hadn't told anyone he had the coke, though he suspected Pook knew what was up. But that didn't matter; they would go on to the park from here, and Dante had already decided that the cocaine wouldn't be coming back. It would be a deal-or-dump thing, and even if he couldn't sell it, at least he wouldn't be spending the rest of his life wishing he'd taken a chance while he still had a choice.

Jinx gave him a grin, but Dante only nodded in return. Jinx was happy. Why not? He finally knew what was "wrong" with himself, and now he had friends. What made it hard for Dante to keep denying him was finding that this slow-witted, slop-bodied boy was really as likable as some squeeze-me-I-squeak-little-kid's toy that you never wanted to hurt. Jinx's grin was defenseless as he pointed with pride to the tag. "You think it cool, Dante? This part I done here?"

Dante resisted the urge to smile and pat Jinx's shoulder, glancing instead at the approaching locomotive. "Yeah. It be all that, man. But, we best bail our asses 'fore we get popped."

Wyatt pulled his camera out of Pook's pack. "Everybody get together first! I want a picture of this! It the flyest thing we ever done!"

The boys grouped a moment in front of the boxcar while Wyatt snapped a picture. Then, in file behind him, they started along the line of railroad cars to go around and out of the yard. But the locomotive's whistle sounded two short toots. Wyatt paused and looked back. "The hell?"

"Um," said Jinx. "Maybe there cops on that engine?"

Pook cocked his head. "Check it. The engineer wavin' to us."

"With all five fingers too," snickered Wyatt.

"Yo," said Dante. "Maybe y'all best keep goin'. Wyatt an' Radgi can't run too good. I go see whattup."

Pook frowned and stepped close, murmuring, "You best not forget what you got in your pack, Dante. You busted with all that shit, they count three strikes an' toss the key!"

Dante forced a casual shrug, muttering low. "So, maybe I get my operation in prison. They get paid to keep you there, so they don't want you dyin' until your time up." He walked away, hearing the crunch of gravel as the other boys continued along the line of cars. The locomotive, two tracks over, had drawn even with the tagged boxcar and came to a stop with a squealing of brakes and blasting of air. The engineer was a white man, but seemed to be smiling. He opened a narrow door in the cab and came out on the catwalk, kneeling at the rail as Dante cautiously neared. Dante pictured himself as he probably looked to the man: moving like a wary little animal in one of those nature shows Wyatt watched, suspicious and ready to run the second something spooked him. He straightened his back and tried putting pride in his stride.

"That's real nice work, son," said the man as Dante stepped up beside the engine.

Dante hadn't known what to expect, but this was about the last thing. He'd talked to very few white people in his life, and then only when he had to. Most were the kind who asked lots of questions but never seemed interested in hearing his answers. "Um. Thanks."

The man's smile seemed natural and not the sort that fronted friendliness like those of the hospital doctors. "My daughter's in college. She's doing some sort of paper on social conditions. She asked me to try to talk to one of you graffiti guys."

Dante cocked his head. "Yeah?"

The man spread heavy-gloved hands. "Well, why do you do it? I see it all over. Some of it's damned ugly, but a lot of it's kind of pretty in a way. Like what you did there." He thought a moment. "Well, *I* think some of it's pretty, anyhow. But it's like a kind of language, isn't it? Except that nobody knows what it means. Is it all gang-related, like they say on TV?" The man studied the boxcar again. "Are you a gang?"

Dante had never considered the concept that any of *them*

might be down with tagging. "Well, no. We be homeys." He paused, wondering why it now seemed important to make this white man understand. "*Some* taggin' done by gangs, but it mostly crap. Gangs don't do cool. Cool taggin' done by *teams*. Y'all see somethin' like what we done there, it . . . well, it be art, what it is. Sorta a . . . statement . . . our *perspective*. TV or cops call that gang-related, they either be fools or lyin' to you."

The man seemed to be thinking, but Dante wondered a moment if this was all a front and he was just trying to stall until the cops came. White faces were hard to read, yet this one seemed somehow more human than most because it showed curiosity instead of suspicion.

The man nodded slowly. "Well, I've had my share of being lied to, son, though I don't suppose you know much about that war in Vietnam. But why are they saying it's all gang-related?"

Dante studied the man's blue eyes, wondering why it always seemed so hard to trust them. "To make you scared of us, so you hate us. That be traditional American values."

The man looked thoughtful and nodded once more. "I guess I am scared . . . scared you were going to say something like that." He raised his eyes to the big bright tag on the rusty old boxcar. "'Nam was kind of pretty too. Beautiful beaches. Nice people if you took the time to get to know them." He sighed. "Though that wasn't what folks back home got to hear." He glanced again at the tag. "'Babylon Boyz.' What's it mean? And, who's 'Willy'?"

Dante turned to study the tag, trying to see it through this man's blue eyes. "Willy our team name, but the other be hard to explain. It kinda mean we trapped. An', we pissed that everybody scared, everybody hatin', but nobody wanna free Willy."

"Mmm." The man nodded once more. "I think you just explained it all right." He smiled again. "And, maybe I understand it better than my daughter will." He rose and leaned on the rail. "Just don't cover up the code strips, okay, son? That's about the only thing I don't like. You guys be careful now."

Dante smiled. "Thanks." He turned and walked away. The other boys were waiting at the end of the line of cars. They reminded him of wary little animals.

"What he say, Dante?" asked Jinx.

"He like art."

Radgi smiled. "I can understand that."

"Mmm," said Wyatt. "Well, where we headed now, they *don't* like art, so everybody be watchin' your brutha's back."

The boys rounded the line of cars and moved across more tracks toward the industrial streets at the eastern side of the rail yard. "Funny," said Pook. "To most of them, it art if it hung in a frame, but a crime if it sprayed on a wall."

Wyatt snickered. "It only a crime if you inhale while you sprayin' it."

The boys passed through a gap in the fence and started for the Lake Merrit BART station. Wyatt was leading as usual, setting the pace. Pook and Jinx walked together. They didn't talk much, but sometimes their hands or arms brushed and they looked at each other and smiled. What they were feeling *couldn't* be any different from "traditional" love, Dante thought. Radgi walked at his side, puffing a little, awkward because of his tummy, but looking happy just the same. Wyatt glanced back once and grinned. "Got you a boyfriend too, Dante?"

"Oh, shut up, fool. You jealous or somethin'?"

They soon reached the station, bought tickets, then went up on the platform to wait for a train. Dante noticed a BART cop eyeing them. In a way it was almost funny: The cop looked as if he was sure they were dirty—maybe packing guns or drugs—and today he was right on all seven. Yet Dante remembered all the times cops had looked at him and his friends the exact same way when they'd been innocent as little angels. It was like, if everyone figured you were dirty, why bother to stay clean?

A train came rumbling in and creaked to a stop. Its doors

sighed open. The boys boarded. Dante sat down with Radgi, while Pook and Jinx took another seat. Wyatt just about filled up a seat all by himself. Dante saw Pook's muscled arm slip naturally over the seat back to encircle Jinx's pudgy shoulders. Anyone could see they cared for each other.

The doors snicked shut and the train purred out of the station. A white voice droned from speakers, telling everybody everything they couldn't do: but boys caring for boys wasn't one of them. Toward the front of the car Dante saw three girls about his own age. He peeped them shyly . . . there was nothing wrong with boys caring for girls either.

They left the train at MacArthur Boulevard station and walked up the street to the park. It was green and well-tended, but a lot of its beauty was lost to the stripped-down and cut-back-for-public-safety look of its bushes and trees. There were people and kids of all colors walking or playing or just sitting on the grass in the midmorning sunlight, though white was the predominant skin color here. Jinx scanned around, more wary and alive today than Dante had ever seen him.

"So, what the plan, Wyatt?"

Wyatt pointed to a small brick maintenance building off in one corner on the Broadway side of the park. "There be our target, kids. Babylon Boyz on the side wall in less'n five. Y'all know the moves. Then we bail our butts in different directions an' hook up back at the BART station."

Radgi looked around. "This's kind of dangerous, ain't it? Tagging up here."

"What it all about, man," said Dante. "Tellin' white folks that them an' their Babylon *ain't* the values the rest of the world gotta live by."

Wyatt gave Dante a long look. "'Member, man, *you* say that 'out no coachin' from me." He scoped the building again. "Won't be nobody round that shady side till the sun move. Me, Pook, an' Jinx do this hit. Dante, Radgi, y'all take our backs. Everybody down?"

Dante thought Radgi looked a little nervous, though he nodded with the rest of the boys.

"Okay," said Wyatt. "Let's do this."

Pook held back as Jinx and Wyatt moved off. "Dante. If shit happen, you get rid of that pack, speed of light! Ain't no green in this world worth gettin' locked in a cage."

Dante frowned. "Most of the time I feel like I be in one already. Don't worry 'bout me."

Pook sighed. "But I do. 'Cause I love you. An', I wish now we just dumped that shit down the toilet the other night."

Dante hesitated, glancing toward Radgi and then taking Pook's arm and leading him a little ways away. "Well . . . I sorta do too, but I gotta do this, Pook. Least I gotta try. It a choice, man, an' it might be our only chance to bail Babylon."

Pook shook his head. "There got to better choices, Dante. Tryin' to buy your way out somethin' always end up hurtin' somebody. An', what about Radgi? You ain't told him nuthin'. You ain't gave *him* a choice if he wanna be in your mix or not. Ain't that the same thing Babylon does?"

Dante gave Radgi an uncertain glance. ". . . I was gonna tell him."

"But you was scared, am I right?" Pook took hold of Dante's shoulders. "You was scared he wasn't gonna like you no more if he found out you was doin' somethin' dirty."

Dante sighed. "I guess so."

"Well, you can't front to your friends, man. Sooner or later they gonna find out who you really are. Maybe they won't like you then, but you gotta give 'em that choice too."

Dante glanced at Radgi again. "It too late to tell him now. But I gonna tell him everything, man. Right after this over."

"Pook!" Wyatt had stopped with Jinx halfway to the maintenance building. "C'mon!"

Dante set his jaw. "Yo. I *gotta* try this, man. It could give us all choices we never had before."

Pook studied Dante, then finally nodded. "Maybe you do. But, *carefully*, brutha. Please."

"POOK!" Wyatt called again.

Dante slipped his arms around Pook, hugging his hard-muscled warmth. "I love you, man." Then he went to Jinx and hugged his sloppy softness, almost really expecting a squeak when he squeezed him. "You be all that, brutha."

Pook and Jinx left to join Wyatt. Dante and Radgi took watch as the other boys assembled behind the building. The hit came off fast and phat. Two small white kids ran over to see, their eyes wide with wonder. Wyatt snapped a quick picture, then the boys all scattered in different directions. Radgi stood in the shade of a tree watching them go, then turned as Dante came over. "Doesn't look like anybody noticed."

Dante scanned the park carefully. "Yeah. An', most of these people don't even know we was part of the team 'cause they don't got a clue how taggin' get done."

"So, do we go back to the station now?"

"Well, wanna just hang here awhile, man? It kinda pretty."

Radgi smiled. "Okay."

Dante took a breath. Pook had been right: It wasn't fair to get Radgi mixed up in this dirty thing. He dug in his pocket for money. "There a store 'cross the street. Go an' score us a ice cream or somethin'. I'ma go to the bathroom. Okay?"

Radgi smiled again. "Sure, Dante . . . um, maybe we can sit over by that pond when I get back? There's some kids with toy boats. We could watch them awhile."

"Uh . . . yeah. That be cool."

Dante watched Radgi walk slowly away, then turned to scan around. Now that he was here, he wasn't sure what to do. The park rest rooms seemed the most likely place for a hookup. He started toward them across the green grass, hearing birdsong in the trees, so different from the harsh screech of seagulls down where he lived. A few people had noticed the tag now: A couple of young high-top African-American types were looking slightly embarrassed, while an older white woman stood scowling at them with suspicion.

Dante kept walking, and each step seemed to bring a clearer realization that he really didn't have clue what to do with the coke. He hadn't been fool enough to figure that some white punk hanging in a park would have that kind of money. But maybe, like Bam-Bam had said, he'd be able to make some sort of contact and get word up the food chain for a fast deal. It would probably be dangerous, and he cursed himself now for selling Air Touch's gun and not borrowing Wyatt's. But he had to do this today. If Jah understood why he was doing it, then maybe He would look the other way . . . at least for a few hours.

Dante scoped carefully around as he neared the bathrooms. He glanced over his shoulder: More people had noticed the fresh tag, but none seemed to connect it to him or Radgi, whose round-tummied little shape was just entering the store across MacArthur Boulevard.

Dante had almost reached the bathrooms now. He could scent strong disinfectant from a morning washdown over the smells of trees and green things. Four white boys about his own age emerged from the doorway. They were dressed hip-hop in baggy jeans and short-sleeved hoodies, but didn't seem like the type who did more than beer or Marlboros. Neither did three Brothers in African attire that looked more like multicolored pajamas. Maybe it was still too early for the dealers to be out.

Dante stopped and looked around once again. All his homeys were gone and he felt scared and alone . . . the perfect victim. He wished that Jah would give him sort of sign. Well, didn't he have free will? What was keeping him from just going into the bathroom and flushing this shit down a toilet?

He glanced up at the sun: It was getting near noon. The other boys were probably at the station by now. He wished he was there too, with Radgi safe at his side. He turned and gazed across MacArthur: Radgi would be back soon with the ice cream. He suddenly wanted to just be a normal kid and sit with Radgi by the pond watching other kids play boats.

He fingered his dreds. Rasta were supposed to care about everybody. Sometimes wearing dreds made you feel like a medic in a war zone. Medics, like doctors, were supposed to help people, not make them sicker. Do No Harm was the code that doctors were supposed to live their lives by. Pook would be a real doctor someday, Dante was almost certain of that, but then what *was* for certain in Babylon? Only that sooner or later it had to come crashing down, and this packful of crap he was carrying was helping to hold it up.

A sign. Please, Jah!

He glanced back across the street again, seeing Radgi with two ice-cream cones, just like a normal kid. Suddenly that was all the sign he needed. He started for the bathrooms. By the time Radgi reached him, the shit would be down the sewer where it belonged that his life would be all clean again.

A big muscle-bulked figure stepped out from behind a tree. Dante froze. It was Air Touch!

"You dirty little nigga!"

Distractedly, Dante noted that Air Touch was dressed in fresh black jeans and T-shirt, his long leather coat hanging open in the heat. Bruises showed on his cheek, and one eye was still slightly puffy. Then, Dante saw Air Touch's right hand, half-concealed by his coat, gripping a big stainless-steel Smith & Wesson.

"Don't you even *think* about runnin', you rag-ass little ho!" hissed Air Touch. "You dead anyways, but gimme that pack an' you might live long enough to tell Jah you comin'!"

Dante felt sweat break out on his body. Desperately, he

looked around, hoping for help. He saw a white family spreading out picnic things on the grass not fifty feet away.

Air Touch shook his head. "Uh-uh, little bitch! You got me in so much shit, it don't matter no more! I cap your ass right here, I got to! Now gimme that pack!"

Dante shot a glance toward MacArthur. Traffic was heavy, and Radgi, burdened by his awkward belly, was waiting for a break to cross the street. There was still a chance to keep him out of this mess.

Air Touch stepped close as Dante fumbled with trembling fingers to slip off the pack straps. "You a stupid mark-ass fool, boy! You *all* nuthin' but stupid snot-nose little niggaboys in this man's world!" He flipped the gun in his hand. "Who you figure afford steel like this?" Air Touch smiled; the same way he'd smiled when pulling his blade on Radgi. "Your little gook friend dead, sucka! I cap his ass right after he tell me how he get my gun an' where you gonna be today! I done *papa-san* too! *That* the kinda power you playin' with, punk!" Air Touch slipped the pack straps over his free arm. "My shit all here?"

Numbly, Dante nodded. Another flick of his eyes showed that Radgi had made it halfway across the street and was now waiting on the center divider. The ice-cream cones were probably starting to melt.

"'Course it is," muttered Air Touch. "The fuck *you* sell product like this!" He smiled again. "Yo. Look like you 'bout ready to have a attack, boy. Better just do it. Get it over with now, an' save yourself the sufferin', 'cause I be comin' back like your worst nightmare to put a bullet through that poor little heart of yours! Just soon's I take care of man's business!" Air Touch's smile widened. "An' I ain't forgettin' your rag-ass little ho, neither!"

Dante had only half-listened to the threats: He'd been living all his life with death as his shadow, and if the Grim Reaper appeared in the guise of a G with a gun instead of a skeleton swinging a scythe, he wouldn't have been much surprised. His next cautious eyeflick showed Radgi trotting clumsily the rest of the way across the street. A car honked, swerving, and Dante wondered if Radgi had just escaped one kind of death only to meet another.

Then, Dante's eyes lifted past Air Touch's shoulder. Two white men had come from behind the bathrooms. Dressed in gray suits, with expensive sunglasses hiding their eyes, they looked like traditional American businessmen, though Dante was somehow sure they were something else. One had sandy-blond hair, the other light brown. Both wore it short. They must have seen what was happening, yet they came over calmly, their shiny black shoes silent on the grass. Dante supposed they were packing their steel in shoulder holsters, yet neither man reached inside their jackets, even when Air Touch noticed where Dante was looking and spun around.

Dante saw Air Touch go tense, but the men came casually on. Cops would have gone for their guns; would have already had them out and gripped in both hands. These men weren't cops; they were way too sure of their power. Dante shot another glance toward the street. Radgi was still far off, but coming steadily closer. Then maybe he saw what was up, because his steps faltered and he stopped. Hand hidden behind him, Dante made a frantic go-away gesture. For a second Dante's heart hammered in his chest when it looked like Radgi would run to him anyway, but then the kid edged toward the shadow of a big clump of bushes. Dante sighed in relief: Radgi had been on the street long enough to recognize danger from a distance.

Air Touch was still facing the approaching men, but seemed to relax just a little. Neither man seemed to have noticed Radgi; they didn't even seem to be paying much attention to the other people around. In fact, they acted as if they owned the whole park and the world it was in.

Dante had seen such men before: uptown, where the big buildings and expensive hotels and restaurants were. They always acted so confident, as if they were the crowns of creation and looked down on everyone else from some higher level. He scented after-shave lotion, soap, and shoe polish. Both men wore watches that looked expensive as hell without seeming showtime. One of the men smiled as if it cost him nothing at all to be nice. "Hello, Air Touch." He seemed amused, pronouncing the name as if it was some funny foreign language used by a primitive race. "You haven't been returning your calls, sport. We were worried about you."

Carefully, Air Touch slipped the Smith & Wesson into the top of his jeans and let his gun arm hang loose at his side. Dante saw him swallow, and just like that night on the waterfront, he could scent the big boy's fear.

". . . I left a message. I tole him what happen. . . . An' I say I take care of it."

The other man smiled. "That was two days ago, sport. He likes to know where his children are." The man studied Dante a moment and one eyebrow lifted slightly. Then he looked back at Air Touch and his tone was like an adult gently teasing a child. "This wouldn't be one of the 'gang' who 'jacked' you, would it?"

Air Touch's voice was a mix of relief and uncertainty. "Yeah! He the dirty little shit stole our product! But I got it covered now! Won't be no more probs!"

The men exchanged brief glances. Dante shot a look toward the bushes. He only saw Radgi because he was looking for him, well-concealed but watching. Dante caught himself wondering for a short stupid second what had happened to the ice-cream cones.

The second man stepped over to Dante and laid a soap-scented hand on his shoulder, then glanced back at Air Touch. "You don't mean to say you're planning to hurt this little guy?"

Air Touch turned around, his eyes widening in something like wonder. ". . . But . . . he *knows!*"

Once more the men exchanged glances; this time they both seemed amused. The first one stretched and yawned, his jacket opening just enough to reveal a glimpse of a snub-nosed Colt in a soft leather holster. "Nice morning, isn't it? Why don't we all go for a ride." The second man gave Dante's shoulder a friendly squeeze. "Want to come along with us, little guy?"

It wasn't really a question.

Air Touch's eyes darted around as if seeking escape, but then he tried to come cool. "Don't worry 'bout him. Nigga can't run away. Gots a bad heart."

Surprisingly, the man knelt in front of Dante. "That true, little guy?"

". . . Yeah. My mom was on crack."

The man rose, shaking his head. "Nasty stuff."

The first man turned to lead the way. Air Touch offered him the pack. "It all here."

The man moved off, not looking back. "You carry it, sport."

The second man followed Air Touch, but walked at Dante's side, one hand staying lightly on Dante's shoulder. Dante risked a last glance back. Seeing Radgi still watching, he made one more quick hand sign to warn the kid off, then faced straight ahead and walked on. He supposed he should be afraid—*very* afraid—but instead he felt only a strange sort of sadness. It was almost the same feeling he'd gotten when the doctors said there was nothing they could do and advised him to make the best of his life. Anyway, what choice did he have? There was no doubt in his mind that either man could catch him in three steps if he did try to run.

They passed the white family picnicking on the grass. The first man nodded pleasantly to them. Dante knew he would find no help there. He was beyond any help now, but at least Radgi had escaped clean.

He caught sight of Air Touch's midnight-black Viper parked at the curb out on Broadway. Behind it was a big new four-doored Lincoln in the sort of soft gray color that hardly got noticed. The first man thumbed what looked like a beeper as they neared, and Dante heard the soft click of locks releasing. Reaching the car, the man opened a back door and held it for Air Touch, whose face and fade were now shiny with sweat. Air Touch was still posing cool, tossing the pack in on the floor, but the man tapped his shoulder. "Better give me the cannon, sport. We're getting out of Dodge."

Air Touch paled a little, but carefully slipped the big gun from his jeans. The man took it the way he'd probably handle a dead rat.

Automatically, Dante moved to get in the back beside Air Touch, but the second man only smiled and squeezed his shoulder once more. "I think you'd better ride up front, little guy. He wants to *hurt* you, remember?"

The man opened the door and Dante got in, settling deep in a seat of soft leather that was almost the same color as his skin. The second man slid in back beside Air Touch, while the first went around and got behind the steering wheel. "Fasten your seat belt, little guy," he said.

Air Touch's voice balanced on the edge of breaking. "My car! The meter run out in a hour! It get towed!"

"Well," said the first man, starting the engine, "there are worse things in the world."

Now that it didn't matter, Dante looked around. He spotted Radgi, who had followed and was now peering from behind a tree at the edge of the park. Maybe he was memorizing the car's license number? But what good would that do? Even if he went to the cops, and even if they would listen to a homeless black hood-rat, Dante suspected that these men were light-years beyond what passed for law in Babylon.

Music murmured from hidden speakers as the Lincoln purred like a big lazy cat up Broadway toward the foothills. To Dante the music sounded like what played all day in the hospital lobby and elevators. The car was air-conditioned, but he wasn't shivering because of that. The driver gave him a glance. "Do you know where we are, little guy?"

Dante looked out the windows, seeing only big beautiful houses with yards of green lawns and nobody around but well-dressed white people. It was like another planet. "Nuh-uh."

The driver's eyes lifted momentarily to the rearview mirror to exchange another glance with the second man.

"He could find his way up here!" blurted Air Touch. "Little shit smarter than he look!"

"He looks a lot smarter than you right now, sport," chuckled the second man.

About the only thing Dante did know for sure was the time: By the clock in the dashboard it was almost exactly a half an hour since leaving the park and cruising ever upward on clean, well-paved streets until the Lincoln came to a stop at a pair of black iron gates set in a six-foot-high white stucco wall. The driver produced his beeper-thing again and the gates swung smoothly and silently open. Dante looked back through the Lincoln's rear window: He could see what was probably all of Oakland, and from way up here he couldn't tell which were the clean parts and which were the dirty. Air Touch's face was still shiny with sweat, even in the coolness of the car. His eyes met Dante's with white-hot rage.

The car rolled up a wide driveway paved with brick as the iron gates swung shut behind. Lawn stretched away on each side, and a flag atop a tall pole hung limp and lifeless like a red, white, and blue bedsheet. Ahead was the sort of huge house that Dante had only seen in movies: pure white like the wall, with a red tile roof and a wide-arched front porch. The car stopped at the steps and the first man again led the way, doing his thing with the beeper to unlock a massive door with carved panels and wrought-iron hinges.

The house like the car was air-conditioned and almost too cold. The first man walked quickly up a long hall walled in spotless white plaster, leaving the second to escort Dante and Air Touch at a slower pace, their footsteps soundless on silver-gray carpet. There were many framed paintings on the walls of pretty places in green country, and Dante was almost sad that he didn't have time to look at them. Through doorways he caught glimpses of beautiful rooms and a kitchen larger than his whole apartment. The house smelled like things instead of people: metal, leather, cloth, and wood. There were no cooking scents in the air. Only Air Touch smelled alive . . . and afraid.

The hallway opened at the end into a huge sunlit room. Its walls too were white, and hung here and there with more paintings of mostly mountains and unspoiled country. Dante wondered if there really were places like that, or maybe they only existed in some artist's mind. One wall was almost all glass and looked out on a turquoise-toned swimming pool that seemed as big as a lake. Sliding doors stood open, and Dante scented chlorine and freshly mowed grass. Bone-white concrete skirted the pool, and beyond was a lush-lawned landscape as large as Dante's school yard and surrounded by a six-foot wall. Somehow the pool and huge yard seemed dead to Dante: Maybe it was because there were no balls or toys or any sign of kids who could play in all this clean space. He wondered if Radgi had ever lived in such a beautiful place when his mother had been rich. If he had, what gave him the courage to go on living after losing it?

"So, *this* is the 'gangster' who caused all the fuss?"

Dante turned. The furniture in the room was all heavy wood and leather. The couches and chairs were the same color as the Lincoln's upholstery . . . the same color as Dante. The first man stood beside another man, who sat in a big recliner that looked like a modern and megaexpensive version of Dante's dad's chair. It was hard to judge white people's ages, but Dante figured this man as being forty or so. He looked something like the others, more well-fed than fat; like the people who played tennis on the

Lake Merrit courts. He was tanned, with short-cut blond hair, and dressed in khaki slacks and safari shirt. He wore those sort of low-top leather sneakers that people with yachts called "deck shoes."

Blue eyes were hard to read, but Dante thought they seemed a little surprised, as if the man had expected the "gangster who caused all the fuss" to be big, buffed, and bad like Air Touch. The eyes lifted a second to signal, and the man who had walked with Dante took the pack from Air Touch and left the room. The man in the chair smiled an unreadable white person's smile and opened a hand toward a couch on his right.

"Come here, son. Sit down. Something to drink? A Coke? Juice? There might be some milk in the refrigerator."

Dante went to the couch and sat down. Everything here was so unreal that it was like a dream in which nothing he did seemed to matter. "Um, can I have a beer?"

The man's eyebrow raised slightly, but he smiled once more. "You might just be needing one. Anchor all right?"

"Um, yes, please."

The first man crossed the room to a small bar in one corner. A minute later he returned and handed Dante a tall glass. Dante had never drank beer from a glass before. It tasted good. He sipped, noting that the man went to stand near and slightly behind Air Touch. Air Touch's eyes shifted uneasily from the man in the chair to Dante. All Dante could think of was that Air Touch probably needed a beer too, but it didn't look like he was going to get one.

The man in the chair turned to Dante, scanning him with a slightly puzzled expression as if he was something entirely new. "A Rastafarian? Or, do you just like dredlocks?"

"Um. Well, I be for real. 'Cept I don't believe in smokin' ganja."

The man cocked his head. "But isn't that part of your religion?"

Dante shrugged. "My dad say Jah already give us a beautiful world, an' we shouldn't gotta smoke somethin' to see it the way He does."

"But didn't Jah put the herb on earth for you to use?"

"My dad say Jah give us hemp to make rope for our boats an' clothes for our backs."

The man's expression turned thoughtful. "Your father must be an interesting man."

"He a good man. I be the one make all the mess."

The second man came back. "One package was opened. Short a gram."

"Um," said Dante. "It was a accident. I didn't snort none."

The man in the chair looked puzzled again. "You seem like a nice young man. How did you get yourself mixed up in this?"

Dante took a big gulp of beer and then sighed. "I . . . need money for a operation."

"Something's wrong with his heart," said the second man.

"My mom was on crack when she had me," Dante added.

The man in the chair almost looked sad, but then his eyes hardened as he turned to Air Touch. "This young man had an accident and lost one gram of product. You . . . *boy* . . . had an 'accident' and lost it all. Accidents happen when boys play games. That's why men make rules. Being on time for the game is one of the rules. . . ."

"But I had to go to a doctor!" cried Air Touch. He gave Dante a murderous glare and shoved back his coat sleeve to show a bandage on his forearm. "Little hood-rat friend of his cut me!"

The man in the chair frowned slightly. "Please don't interrupt me again." His frown deepened. "And if a 'little hood-rat' could damage you, then you're a *very* poor player. The fact remains that you dropped the ball, leaving it for anyone to pick up, and ran off to play some little boy's game. Then I had to send a lot of men — men who really have much more important things to do — out looking for you."

"But, I got the shit back!"

The man looked patient, but sighed. "If you had played by the rules, you'd never have lost the product in the first place. You knew the game plan, yet you took off on your own. . . ."

"But, I tole you why! Cops was after me!"

Again the man sighed, and this time he shook his head. "Well, I've tried to put this in terms I thought you could understand. We easily could have recovered the product. . . ."

"From the *cops?*"

For a second the man looked annoyed, but then a slight smile twitched his lips. "It's not widely advertised, but quite of few of them play on our team." Then he frowned. "And you've interrupted me again. For the third time. Still, I suppose your mother did her best." He thought a moment. "Well, we've wasted enough time on this."

Air Touch's eyes went wide and confused. The man in the chair nodded to the one beside Air Touch, who slipped the big Smith & Wesson from his waistband and cocked the hammer. Air Touch paled and started to back away, but the man reversed the gun and offered it. Hesitantly, eyes flicking from one man to the other and then to the one in the chair, Air Touch took it. The man in the chair beckoned with a finger. Air Touch approached him, the gun muzzle-down at his side. Dante watched, suddenly tense, clutching the beer glass in both hands.

"Kill the boy."

"NOOOO!" Spilling the beer, Dante cringed back in the soft leather cushions. His arms flew up to try to cover his face. He saw Air Touch grin in triumph . . . saw the gun muzzle big as a sewer pipe aimed at his heart.

CLICK.

Dante blinked. Air Touch's eyes seemed to glaze in amazement. They dropped to the gun, but then went hard again. He gripped the gun to cock it.

The man in the chair sounded bored. "Don't bother, boy, it's not loaded." He turned to Dante, who was cowering on the couch and trying to fight tears. "See how it is with your people, son? I told him to kill you and he didn't hesitate for a second. Can you still believe in the love of Jah after that?"

Dante sucked deep breaths, trying to quiet his heart and stop his body from shaking. A tear slid down his cheek and he wiped it away. The crotch of his jeans was wet, but he was thankful to find it was only spilled beer. "Jah give us free will," he managed to whisper.

"Mmm. So He did, son." The man gestured to the other, who stepped up and took the gun from Air Touch's limp fingers. Dante's eyes followed Air Touch's, watching as the man pulled the magazine and slipped in a single bullet. Sunlight ripples from the pool wavered across the ceiling, glinting on the gun's shiny steel as the man locked the magazine in place and cocked the hammer once more. As if in a dream, Dante saw the gun being offered to him.

That must be it! he thought suddenly. This whole thing had to be a dream! He was sleepwalking again, and Jah had taken his hand to show him the way! Any second now Radgi would wake him up and they'd sit by the pond eating ice-cream cones!

"Take it, son." The voice was soft, but not Jah's.

And this was no dream. Slowly, Dante obeyed. He seemed powerless not to. He saw Air Touch cringe back, just as he had done, but both the standing men grabbed the big boy's arms and forced him to his knees in front of Dante. Air Touch was strong, but he might have been just a child in the white men's hands. He struggled, but they held him down. He looked desperately to the man in the chair.

"You can't! . . . He TELL!"

The man shrugged. "And just *who* will he tell, this little stranger in a strange land? Besides, he needs to learn a valuable lesson, and you, my boy, are the teaching material." He turned to Dante and pointed. "The forehead, son. It's messy, but quick."

Dante gripped the heavy gun in both hands. He realized that

the last time he'd held it this way, it had been aimed at Wyatt. "No! I ain't gonna!"

The voice was patient once more: an adult explaining how the world worked to a child. "Of course you will, son. You have no choice. He isn't going to let you live now, whatever happens. He *can't,* son. He hasn't got free will anymore. He sold it a long time ago when he signed up to play in the game that you people seem to think you invented." The man studied Dante. "What if I said that only one of you can leave this room alive? If you don't kill him now, I'll give him back the gun. What do you think he'll do?"

Dante's eyes locked on Air Touch's, seeing a faint spark of hope, but also the answer to the white man's question. A sigh escaped Dante, disguised as a sob. He took aim . . .

And spit in Air Touch's face.

The men holding Air Touch tensed and dropped him, their hands diving into their jackets, but Dante pulled gently on the trigger, thumbs on the hammer, letting it soundlessly down. One of the men took the gun, a troubled expression on his face. Once again Dante looked into the eyes of the big black boy on the floor. What he saw there didn't frighten him anymore; it only made him sad.

Then, the man in the chair gave a nod. It happened almost too fast to follow. One of the other men pulled out his Colt. There was a gun blast. Crimson spray burst from the side of Air Touch's skull, spewing across the silver-gray carpet. The boy's big body jerked sideways, slamming down on the floor, twitching and quivering.

Dante sat frozen in horror. The gunpowder smell burned his nostrils. Through ears numbed by the shot, he heard the man in the chair:

"See? You killed him anyway, son."

Slowly, Dante faced the man. The scent of blood made his mouth dry and salty. He had to swallow to get the words out:

"No. You did."

The man only looked thoughtful once more. He rose from the

chair and stepped around what lay on the carpet. Then he turned to the other men and jerked a thumb at Dante.

"Take him back where you found him."

The man walked to the doorway, but stopped and turned again, facing Dante. "Free will isn't free, son. You pay for it every time you make a choice. And even if you choose not to choose, you've still made a choice."

"Boy!"

Dante looked up to see a fat white cop glaring down at him. It was almost a surprise to find himself sitting on grass, his back to a tree. The sunlight in the park had taken on the golden glow of late afternoon. The air was hot and drowsy, and the drone of bees among flowers carried over the city sounds. Nearby was an anthill; little black living things busy with their own world and not knowing they were part of a bigger one. Dante supposed he'd been watching them, but he wasn't sure why. Glancing again at the cop, he put on his pouty-lion look, seeming stupid and sullen to the man.

"Yeah?"

The cop aimed a finger toward the maintenance building. "You know anything about that mess?"

Dante shrugged. "What mess?"

"The mess on that wall, goddamnit!"

Dante looked over at the BABYLON BOYZ tag, now bright in sunlight. "No."

The cop made a disgusted sound. "Yeah. Sure you don't! Get up! Empty that pack!"

Dante stood, picking his pack off the ground, ripping Velcro and turning it upside down. Only a fool wouldn't have already seen it was empty, but the cop snatched it and shook it hard. "What's your name?"

"Willy."

"Where do you live?"

"Babylon."

The cop grabbed Dante's arm and glanced quickly around to see if anyone was near. "Don't smart-mouth me, nigger! You're just reading that off the wall! Now, where do you live?"

Sighing, Dante named a street not far from his home. The cop scowled and let him go, dropping the pack on the grass. "Then you got no business here! Get your little black ass back where you belong!"

The cop turned and stalked off, crushing ants underfoot. Dante turned toward the tag again, watching the mix of expressions on the people pausing to look at it. Then he glanced past the starkly trimmed trees. Out on Broadway, a tow truck was hooking up Air Touch's Viper. Dante brushed back his dreds, shouldered his pack, and started toward MacArthur.

"Dante!"

Dante shaded his eyes with his hand and squinted into the sunglare. Radgi came running clumsily to him, gasping for breath. The kid's shirt was soaked with sweat, and droplets glittered like molten copper in woolly-wild hair beneath the greasy old X cap. Behind Radgi came Pook, Jinx, and Wyatt, all shirtless and gleaming. Radgi stumbled up to Dante, fear in big bronze-green eyes. "What happened? . . . Air Touch . . . an', those men . . . ?"

Radgi swayed, and Dante caught him under the arms. Pook ran up, and together they lowered Radgi to the grass. Dante dropped to his knees at Radgi's side. "Radgi! You okay?"

Radgi managed a weak smile, still gasping. "Yeah."

Pook wiped sweat from Radgi's forehead. "Chill, man. Just lay there till you get your breath back." He turned to Dante. "Radgi run all the way home to get us! What happen?"

Wyatt plopped down in a roly-poly heap beside Radgi. "Yeah! Radgi say Air Touch an' some white men take you away in a car!"

Jinx gripped Dante's shoulder. "Kelly an' his father dead! We thought Air Touch gonna try an' kill you too!"

"The hell happen, Dante?" Pook demanded again.

Dante didn't answer right away. He stayed on his knees beside Radgi, seeing the caring kind of love in the eyes all around him. "Choices happen," he murmured.

Wyatt had noticed the tow truck, now driving off with the Viper hooked like a dead thing behind. He nudged Pook and pointed, then faced Dante. "What happen to Air Touch?"

Dante shrugged. "He made a bad choice. Like a little black ant, he got stepped on." Dante looked around at the faces of his friends and then smiled at Radgi. "Let's go home."

The sun had lowered toward evening, its light growing rosy as the boys reached Dante's house and wearily climbed the front steps. Radgi seemed exhausted: he'd been leaning on Dante all the way home. Wyatt unlocked the door, and Dante helped Radgi up the staircase as Pook and Jinx followed.

"Um, Dante?" called Wyatt, staying below and panting almost as hard as Radgi. "Want me to snag us some beer?"

"That be cool, man."

In the apartment, Radgi stumbled to the couch and collapsed. The kid's brilliant brown complexion seemed pale. Dante gave Pook a worried glance. Pook spread helpless hands in return.

"Here, Radgi," said Dante, unfolding the blanket. "Lay down, man. Chill. Ain't nuthin' to worry 'bout no more."

Radgi's face brightened a little as Dante spread the blanket. "Thanks."

Dante stripped off his pack and sank down in his dad's chair. He felt as worn out as Radgi looked, but then had a thought. "Jinx. Turn on the TV?"

"Oh, sure."

Jinx went over and clicked the knob. The evening news was on. Pook gave Dante a glance, showing he knew what was up, then sat down on the floor in front of the coffee table with Jinx to watch. The world hadn't changed: two boys at some white-bread school had been expelled for holding hands on campus in defiance of traditional American values and wouldn't be allowed to attend their eighth-grade graduation. A BART cop who had killed an unarmed fourteen-year-old black boy for "running away" was back on the force with congratulations for a job well done, and a church group who believed in "the right to life" had firebombed a family-planning center, killing a doctor.

Wyatt came in with a six-pack of Rolling Rock just as there was a fifteen-second mention of a Korean liquor store owner and his son found murdered early that morning. Dante took the bottle Wyatt offered and drank deep. The news ended. Dante suspected there would never be anything about Air Touch. The TV never told what really happened behind the big movie set called Babylon.

Dante got up and went over to sit on the arm of the couch. He gazed down at Radgi, whose eyes were half-closed and seemed far away. "Um, you okay, man? You don't look so good."

Radgi's breath was still ragged. His big eyes seemed uncertain, but a small brown hand closed over Dante's. "I think so."

Suddenly the kid's eyes flew wide in something like horror. "I gotta go to the bathroom!"

Then, Dante gaped in amazement as a big wet stain spread through the blanket below Radgi's stomach. For a second Dante could only stare, then he jumped up. "Pook! He . . . wet himself!"

The other boys scrambled to their feet, crowding around the couch as Radgi moaned and burst into tears. But Pook shoved them all aside, grabbing the blanket and flinging it away.

Radgi's jeans and the cushion beneath were soaking wet. The scent in Dante's nostrils was warm and steamy and somehow familiar. Radgi still clutched his hand, but Dante could only stand staring. Pook's eyes went to slits, and he scowled and shook his head. "Fool!" he muttered.

Dante's mouth dropped open. *"Me?"*

Pook shot Dante a furious glance, ignoring Jinx and Wyatt, who also stood staring. "No, damnit, ME! Everythin' was right there in the book all the time an' I didn't even see it! Some kinda 'doctor' I be!" He bent over and began to unbutton Radgi's Levi's.

Radgi struggled weakly to stop him. "No!"

"The hell goin' on?" demanded Wyatt.

"Shut up!" bawled Pook. "Everbody get back! Gimme some goddamn room!" He undid the last button and peeled the wet jeans from below Radgi's belly.

"No!" Radgi moaned again.

Pook frowned. "You shut up too, fool. It way past frontin' time! Why didn't you just tell us?"

Wyatt's eyebrows shot up as Pook pulled the jeans gently down Radgi's brown legs. Now Jinx's jaw dropped. Dante gaped again in shock. "He . . . he a *girl!*"

"*She*, man," muttered Pook. "Girls is always 'she.'" He untied Radgi's Adidas, slipped off the sodden SilverTabs, and threw them away. "An', she gonna have a baby!"

"Wemarkabo!" Wyatt leaned forward in interest, while Jinx backed away and stumbled against the coffee table.

Dante swallowed. "Oh . . . hell!"

Radgi still clung to Dante's hand. Dante swallowed again, staring at Radgi and wondering why he'd never questioned what now seemed so clear: a face more pretty than handsome, never without a shirt, and keeping the cap on to look more boyish. "Are . . . you gonna have it now?"

Radgi's eyes searched the others around her and she seemed reassured at what she saw. Her own went to Pook. "Am I?"

Pook thought a moment. "Well, this be just your water breakin', Radgi. It only the beginnin'. Y'all could have the baby in a hour, or could be all night. We ain't gonna know much more till you start havin' contractions."

"What are those?"

"Believe, homegirl, you *know* when you get 'em."

Radgi gripped Dante's hand tighter as she scanned Pook's face. "Will they hurt?"

"Well . . . yeah. But, I guess they s'posed to. My book say it part of the 'sacred joy of motherhood.'"

"Bet that book was wrote by a man," muttered Wyatt. "Just axe my mom."

"Oh, shut up!" snapped Pook. "S'prised you wasn't in the *National Enquirer* as the world's biggest baby! Go tell your mom to call a ambulance."

"NOOOOO!"

Radgi's sudden scream sent ice down Dante's spine. The girl's small fingers clamped on his hand so tight he felt the bones creak. Her teeth bared in a snarl, and her whole body arched rigid for a long, painful moment.

"Uh . . . I guess that was a distraction," said Jinx. He plopped heavily down on the coffee table.

Tears filled Radgi's eyes. She gasped for breath, but held on to Dante's hand. "No! Please! If I got to a hospital, they'll just lock me up again! Dante, let me have my baby here with you! *Please!* My mom said our people have babies all the time without hospitals!"

"Cool!" cried Wyatt. "I'ma go get my camera!"

"Shut up!" yelled Pook. He knelt beside the couch. His strong bronze hands moved slowly over Radgi's big brown belly, pressing gently here and there, fingers feeling the new life inside. "How long you been pregnant, Radgi?"

". . . I'm not sure. For a while I just thought I was getting fat. Then I started throwing up in the morning . . . an' then, one day, I felt it move."

"Well, when did . . ." Pook reconsidered. "What I axin' is, how many times . . ." He frowned. "Yo. Y'all *do* know how babies made, don't you?"

Radgi's eyes went to Dante's for a second, but then shied

away, seeming uneasy. "It was only once. Last fall. Right after I ran away."

Pook cocked his head. "In September?"

". . . Yeah. I remember how strange it seemed; kids going to school and I couldn't."

Pook counted on his fingers. "September, October . . . it June now, so that be nine months. A normal term."

Dante had leaned close to Radgi, wondering why she wouldn't meet his eyes. Then he said softly, "It just sorta . . . happened, huh?"

Radgi closed her eyes and nodded. "After I was on the street, I found out real fast it was safer to be a boy. But, at first, I made a lot of mistakes. It was hard pretending to be something I wasn't." She wiped at her eyes, now glistening with tears. ". . . He . . . started watchin' me. One night he found out where I was sleeping. He . . . made me do it. I didn't have a choice."

Dante squeezed the girl's hand. "It cool, Radgi. Lotta things happen we don't got no choices about."

"Yo," said Wyatt. "If she gonna have the baby here, I get to take pitchers!"

"Shut up, man," said Dante, "or I kick your ass out. This be serious shit!"

Jinx rose from the table and came close, touching Pook's shoulder. "Um, would it be safe if she had it here?"

"Ain't nuthin' in Babylon ever been 'safe,' brutha." Pook glanced at Dante again. "'Cordin' to the book, everythin' normal so far. Baby 'bout in the right position. One contraction already. An', Radgi be strong."

"So, I go get my camera," said Wyatt.

Dante scowled. "If you say that again, I go upside your head, fool!" He faced Pook. "But what if somethin' go wrong?"

"I want to have it here!" cried Radgi, clutching Dante's hand even tighter.

Pook nodded. "It cool, Radgi. . . . Dante, go an' put clean sheets on your bed."

"But . . ."

"Look, man, what it is. Radgi gonna freak, goin' to a hospital. Attitude mean a lot when you havin' a baby."

Dante's eyes went from Radgi's to Pook's. "But, this be *real,* man. It ain't playin' doctor."

Pook stood up, looking somehow older. "When I ever *play* doctor? Radgi wasn't here with us now, she prob'ly be havin' her baby behind a Dumpster while the rats watch."

"Pook can do it!" said Radgi.

"'Course he can," Jinx agreed.

"So?" demanded Wyatt. "*Now* can I go get my camera?"

Dante scowled again. "Shut the . . ."

"It's okay," said Radgi. "Let him."

"Cool!" Wyatt lumbered for the door. Pook bent down to Radgi again. "Here, girl, I help you up. Dante, get them sheets changed now!"

"Um?" asked Jinx. "What about boilin' water, Pook? In the movies, people always boil water when they havin' a baby."

"Oh, sure. Go boil lots of water."

Dante paused in the hallway. "Um, *why* do people always boil water, Pook?"

"So the doctor can wash his hands, fool."

Radgi took Pook's hand. "Is that really why?"

"Well, y'all need nice clean water for washin' the baby in." Pook patted Radgi's hand, then trotted over to catch Dante in the hall. He lowered his voice. "Get all the clean sheets in the house, man. Havin' a baby can sorta make a mess."

A few minutes later, Radgi lay naked on Dante's bed in the little turret room. Dante came in with an armful of sheets. Jinx was in the kitchen, tending four big pans of water on the stove. Pook sat by the bedside with his medical book, studying it carefully while trimming his fingernails. Radgi's brilliant brownness seemed to glow against the white linen. She smiled at Dante, reaching for his hand as he set down the sheets and came over. Droplets of sweat glistened on her forehead.

"I just had another contraction. Pook's timing them. He's got everything covered."

Dante took Radgi's hand and smiled back. "'Course he does." Dante looked into Radgi's eyes. "I wish you'd trusted me. What I sayin' is, I like you even better bein' who you really are."

"You can take off my cap again, if you want."

"I think you kinda pretty with it on."

Pook looked up from his book. "Yo, Dante! Got any string?"

"String? Um, there some on my kite in the closet."

"That do. Cut me two pieces. 'Bout a foot long. Go boil 'em. An', boil this box knife too."

Dante started for the closet, but Radgi's back arched in another contraction. Dante ran to her, taking her hand again, but she bit her lip this time, not making a sound. When it was over, she sank back on the pillow, panting. "Want me to push, Pook? Like you were saying?"

Pook glanced at the bedside clock. "Not yet. Wait till I tell you. Pull your legs up, it better like that."

Wyatt came puffing in with his camera. Seeing Radgi on the bed, he snapped a picture. Dante scowled. "Stop screwin' around, man! Yo! Go get two pieces of string off my kite an' boil 'em! An', boil that knife too!"

Pook looked up again. "Then get all the pillowcases an' towels you can find! An' white T-shirts! Boil 'em. Then bring me a pan of warm water."

"Well, okay," said Wyatt, setting the camera on Dante's desk, "but call me if somethin' cool happen."

Dante helped Pook lift Radgi so that her back was braced against a pile of pillows. Another contraction came. This time she took it knees up and straining, with Pook holding tight to her ankles and Dante gripping her hand. Wyatt came back with an armload of steaming linen, grabbed his camera, and took another picture. Radgi sank down panting for breath, her body gleaming with sweat.

"That was a good one," said Pook.

Radgi forced a small smile. "If that . . . was a good one, I hope . . . I don't have a bad one!" She turned to Dante. "That's sort of how you looked when you had your attack."

Wyatt snickered. "So, he kinda know what the 'sacred joy of motherhood' feel like!"

Jinx appeared in the doorway. "The water all boiled, Pook."

"Then get it in here. . . . Wyatt, wash your hands. I maybe gonna need help."

"Cool!"

"What about me?" Dante demanded.

"Get a washcloth an' wipe Radgi's face, then just hold her hand. That a important thing to do."

Radgi's face paled again. "H-here comes another one . . . AAAAH!" Suddenly, with amazing strength, she pulled Dante's hand to her mouth.

"OW! She *bit* me!"

Pook shrugged. "Give her a licorice stick. Bitin' a normal thing to do. It say in the book even women of good breedin' bite."

"Damnit!" said Wyatt. "I missed the picture!"

Radgi pressed Dante's hand, then kissed it. "I'm sorry."

Pook bent over the bed, all muscles and maleness but moving his hands gently over Radgi's stomach. "Not much longer now. This be a textbook birthin'. . . . Jinx! Where that goddamn water?"

Jinx reappeared, lugging pans. Dante dashed to his desk and snagged a piece of licorice, then returned to the bed and slipped the stick between Radgi's teeth before taking her hand once more. Pook laid out the two pieces of boiled string and the box knife on the night table. Radgi's back arched again, and Pook grabbed her ankles. Wyatt readied his camera.

"AAAAAAH!"

Sweat gleamed on Pook's own body as he struggled to hold the girl. "Jinx! Wyatt! Take her feet!"

The boys took hold, and Pook reached between Radgi's legs. "Push! *Now,* girl!"

"AAAAAAAAAH . . . AAAAH!"

"Not *that* hard! You don't gotta shoot it 'cross the room!"

"Whoa!" cried Jinx. "I can see the baby's head!"

Holding to Radgi's ankle with one hand, Wyatt snagged his camera with the other and snapped another picture.

"It goin' back inside!" yelled Jinx. "Pook! Can't you pull it out?"

"Shut up! Y'all don't go yankin' a baby into the world! You see what waitin' out here, *you* wanna get back inside where it safe, too! One more time, Radgi. *Push!*"

Again, the girl strained, sobbing, biting hard on the licorice. Dante wiped her face with the cloth, staring in wonder as a little brown baby emerged. It seemed to be wrapped in cellophane. There was blood, but not much.

"Wemarkabo!" said Wyatt. His camera clicked again.

Radgi sank back against the pillows once more, gasping but watching as Pook gathered the baby up in a towel. Her eyes turned to Dante. "I . . . really . . . made a . . . mess . . . huh?"

Dante gave her hand a squeeze. "It a nice clean mess."

"There still the afterbirth comin'," said Pook. "Dante. Get the string. Tie the cord here. Tight. 'Bout three inches from the little . . . *brutha's* . . . tummy." Carefully, Pook cleaned the baby's face and mouth, while Dante tied the string tight around the umbilical cord. Wyatt busied himself snapping pictures.

"Um?" asked Jinx. "Ain't you s'posed to hold it upside down an' whack its bottom?"

"How *you* like gettin' whacked first thing on earth? Ain't no wonder kids start out with a attitude." Pook rocked the baby in his hard-muscled arms. It suddenly let out a squall. "Guess he just figure out what kinda world he come into." Pook laid the baby between Radgi's legs. "Dante. Gimme the other piece of string. Jinx. Get the knife."

Dante moved back to Radgi's side, taking her hand again, watching as Pook tied the second piece of string about an inch from the first, then cut the cord between them with the box knife blade. Wyatt snapped a last picture.

Radgi reached out. "Can I hold him now, Pook?"

"In a minute. We gotta wait for the afterbirth. Dante, wash the baby with the warm water." Pook washed his own hands, dried them on a T-shirt, then closed the book and laid it on Dante's desk. "Jinx. Wyatt, When the afterbirth come, we clean everythin' up an' let Radgi rest."

When it was over, Radgi lay back with the baby cradled to her small, soft breasts. Dante stood at the bedside. He smiled, remembering that he'd once thought her to be just a chubby-chested boy. Jinx and Wyatt cleaned up the room and carried things out. Dante took Radgi's hand once more. "You rest now, like Pook say. An' don't worry 'bout nuthin'. My dad be home tomorrow, we figure out what to do. Ain't nobody gonna be lockin' you up in no state-sponsored suckhole."

Wyatt paused in the doorway, his arms full of wet sheets and linen. "Well, my mom all the time sayin' how she always want a girl." He grinned. "An', it don't look like she gonna get Pook."

Dante met Radgi's eyes. "Wyatt's mom cool. Want him to bring her up now?"

Radgi sighed, cradling her baby. "I guess we have to start thinkin' ahead, don't we?"

"Yeah, Radgi. We do."

Pook nodded. "Go get your mom, Wyatt."

The fat boy waddled away. Radgi closed her eyes, the baby

nuzzling her breast and making soft sounds. Dante turned to leave, but Radgi reached for his hand. For a moment it seemed like she would cry again. "Dante, this is Air Touch's baby."

Dante gave Pook a glance, but then smiled at the girl. "No, Radgi, he be *your* baby."

He held Radgi's hand. Life wouldn't be easy. Maybe it never would. But there were choices, and it was better when you had friends to help make the right ones. There *was* a way out of Babylon, but you had to have perspectives to find it. He bent down and kissed Radgi's forehead, and then kissed the tiny brown boy in her arms.